CHAUCER'S CANTERBURY TALES
IN BITE-SIZE VERSE

By the same author:

Kenneth Grahame's The Wind in the Willows in Bite-Size Verse, The Book Guild, 2005

Easy Reading Shakespeare Volume One: The Bard in Bite-Size Verse, The Book Guild, 2005

Easy Reading Shakespeare Volume Two: The Bard in Bite-Size Verse, The Book Guild, 2006

Easy Reading Shakespeare Volume Three: The Bard in Bite-Size Verse, The Book Guild, 2006

CHAUCER'S CANTERBURY TALES

In Bite-Size Verse

Richard Cuddington

Book Guild Publishing

Sussex, England

First published in Great Britain in 2008 by
The Book Guild Ltd
Pavilion View
19 New Road,
Brighton,
BN1 1UF

Typesetting in Times by
Keyboard Services, Luton, Bedfordshire

Printed in Great Britain by
Antony Rowe Ltd, Chippenham, Wiltshire

A catalogue record for this book is available from
The British Library

ISBN 978 1 84624 246 5

For Julia

CONTENTS

A Miller sought to ride with us –
Immense in brawn and bone

THE PROLOGUE

When April showers fall and shed
New life on every flower,
Ending the drought of March – well then
There comes a hallowed hour

When people's hearts become engaged
And longingly combine
To make their way as pilgrims do
To Canterbury's shrine;

To where the holy martyr died,
At Christ's cathedral there,
They seek his help to cure all ills
And wipe away all care.

Thus it was at Southwark's inn,
The Tabard, one fine day,
I dwelt with patience and resolve –
Prepared to make my way

To Canterbury – on pilgrimage,
Made ready to depart
Upon my holy journey with
A most impassioned heart.

That night as I stayed at the inn
It then came to befall
That nine and twenty others came –
True pilgrims, one and all.

And they were all intent like me
To make their eager way
To Canterbury – we'd all set out
Upon the following day.

But I'll take time before we leave
To say a word or two
About the people gathered there,
About this motley crew.

I'll tell you first about a KNIGHT,
A man, whom all there swore,
Had done his duty fair and square
In his dear sovereign's war.

He'd fought so many battles
In many a foreign land,
And he'd been honoured countless times –
He was a real firebrand.

He'd fought in Alexandria,
In Lithuania too,
In Africa and Russia,
In Europe, through and through.

This Knight was held in high esteem
In everybody's eyes,
So splendid in his bearing – so
Compassionate and wise.

He'd never said a boorish thing
And lies could not invade
His noble mind – his manner was
That of a modest maid.

He'd always been an honest soul
Doing what was right,
Throughout his life he'd tried to be
A true and perfect knight.

His handsome son was with him too,
A fine and manly SQUIRE,
A brave young lad of twenty years
Whose frame was all a-fire

With thoughts of chivalry and love –
They lit his youthful face,
He hoped in time that he would gain
A certain lady's grace.

He knew just how to joust and dance
And how to draw and write,
And he would make up poems which
He'd expertly recite.

And in the cavalry he'd served
Where he had proved to be
Bold and gallant – fighting in
Artois and Picardy.

A YEOMAN stood there at his side
Dressed in a coat of green,
He carried arrows quite as sharp
As any ever seen.

And in his hand he held with pride
A long and supple bow
Which he had used with great panache
To fight his country's foe.

He knew the art of woodcraft,
A forester – and more,
For he could be relied upon
In peace and time of war.

A lady also joined us there
Who from her simple dress,
Confirmed she was a holy Nun,
In fact – a PRIORESS.

She had a way of smiling,
So modest and so coy,
And when she chose to make an oath,
She made it 'By St. Loy'.

Her name was Madam Eglentyne,
'En Français' she would speak,
Her accent, sadly, in this tongue
Was really rather weak.

More of the school of Stratford
Than Paris to the ear,
Her intonation wasn't right,
It sounded trite, I fear.

Her table manners were refined
For I must here relate,
No morsel from her lips would fall
When this good lady ate.

No dish however greasy
Could ever foil or beat her,
All in the company agreed
She was a dainty eater.

And once she'd finished she would wipe
Her upper lip so clean
To make quite sure that not a trace
Of grease was ever seen.

She had a very friendly way,
Her heart was soft as butter,
And kindly words were all that she
Was ever heard to utter.

A MONK was there as well and he
Was plump and bald of head,
And he was dressed in clothes of quite
The most expensive thread.

It was apparent that his tastes
Were lavish and immense,
In everything it seemed that he
Just wouldn't spare expense.

This was a man who loved his life,
He loved his food and wine,
And falconry and hunting too –
For him life was just fine.

In contrast to this Monk there was
A FRIAR – a merry soul,
Just bringing joy to other folk
Was this man's only goal.

He was renowned for singing
And happily was blest
With a voice that all agreed
Was really quite the best.

But he was poor, indeed he was
A Limiter, which meant
He had the right to freely beg
To pay for food and rent.

He was a first-class beggar too,
The finest of his batch,
There just was no-one to compare –
His skills were hard to match.

And to secure his district
He paid a certain rent
Which made quite sure no other Friar
Frequented where he went.

So when it came to begging
He really was a star,
He could get cash from anyone –
He was the best by far.

And though a lowly widow
Might be short of a shoe
He'd get a farthing from her with
A pleasant how d'you do.

And with the wealthy folk as well
He'd be the very same,
He was a wily, artful Friar
And Hubert was his name.

A MERCHANT also joined us there,
He had a beard that forked,
His highly polished, buckled boots
Shone brightly as he walked.

He talked in solemn overtures
As on his horse he sat,
His dress was stylish – colourful,
He wore a beaver hat.

He gave the strong impression that
His finances were set
In goodly state of order but
In truth he was in debt.

Despite this fact he really was
A sound type all the same,
Quite the best of fellows but
I do not know his name.

A CLERK from Oxford was resolved
To come with us and make
The pilgrimage – the horse he rode
Was thinner than a rake.

He wasn't very fat himself,
He had a sober stare,
The coat he wore it must be said
Was really quite threadbare.

For he believed that knowledge
Was life's important key
And so he spent his money on
Books of philosophy.

He'd never overeat or take
Pleasure from a bottle,
His greatest joy was just to read
The works of Aristotle.

To study was his passion,
His solitary yearning,
And so he lived his life enmeshed
Within a web of learning.

He never spoke without good cause –
He'd never seek a quarrel,
But when he spoke you could be sure
His message would be moral!

A SERGEANT OF THE LAW came too,
A man well known and wise,
For many years he'd held the post
Of Justice of Assize.

He knew the details off by heart
Of every case and crime
Going back for countless years
Right to King William's time.

He could defend with skill and verve
And write out legal screeds,
And quote the law on anything
And draft out perfect deeds.

So in short it's fair to say
He really knew his stuff,
And with these observations made
I think I've said enough.

A FRANKLIN there was set to come
To Canterbury too,
This was a man who owned some land
And thus he did accrue

A certain level of respect
As true freeholders can,
But sad for him he could not claim
To be a nobleman.

This was a man whose every act
Was sanguine and benign,
He loved all forms of pleasure and
He loved to quaff his wine.

His house was full to bursting point
With fowl and meat and fish
Of quite the finest quality
Ensuring every dish

That graced his table was the best
That cash could ever buy,
His pantry overflowed with food –
His cellar ne'er ran dry.

Woe to the cook if food was served
Unsalted in a pot,
Or dished out to his guests with sauce
That wasn't really hot.

In his great hall he always had
A table fully laid
In case an unexpected call
By a friend was made.

Justice of Sessions he had been
And Member for the Shire,
And so within his county there
Nobody had stood higher.

Also amongst the company
Were tradesmen, good and true,
A DYER and a CARPENTER,
A CARPET-MAKER too.

A HABERDASHER also came,
A WEAVER there as well,
They all seemed Christian and devout
As far as one could tell.

They all looked spick and span and trim,
And each of course was skilled
Within his trade – and proud to be
A member of his Guild.

A COOK had come along with them,
A man of some renown,
For he could tell just by a sip
The ale from London town.

And when he cooked a chicken – well
Its flavour stood alone,
His roasts and soups were quite the best
That anyone had known.

This man could cook in any way,
He'd boil and bake and fry,
And turn out anything from bread
To meat or apple pie.

But such a pity, I must say,
Or so it seemed to me,
For this poor fellow suffered from
An ulcer on his knee.

A SHIPMAN was to join us too,
From Dartmouth he did hail,
A naval man who'd spent his life
Living under sail.

He rode a tired, old farmer's horse
And wore a woollen gown,
The summer sun had tanned his skin
The colour of nut-brown.

He'd fought in many battles and
When victory was assured,
The normal rules of winning – why –
He'd studiously ignored.

For when a rival ship was holed,
He'd watch it as it sank,
And all survivors from the ship
He'd force to walk the plank.

His knowledge was unequalled
On winds and reefs and tides,
On currents, weather and the stars
And so much more besides.

For he knew every cove and bay
And sound, safe havens there,
From Gotland in the north right to
The Cape of Finisterre.

He knew the bays of Brittany,
The creeks and coves of Spain,
And the barque he owned was called
The good ship 'Maudelayne'.

There was a DOCTOR with us too –
Nobody quite like he,
An expert on all medicines
And points of surgery.

He was convinced that he possessed
The most amazing powers,
Conscientious to a fault,
He'd tend the sick for hours.

In everything, he was well versed,
This man was never thrown,
And he was up to speed on all
Hippocrates had known.

And with great ease he'd diagnose
Every bad condition,
He really was a first-class chap,
A truly great physician.

A worthy WOMAN FROM BATH town
Was set to come along,
Despite the fact we really were
A most unlikely throng.

At making cloth she was the best,
She had a special bent,
For she was better at her trade
Than craftsmen out of Ghent.

Within the parish where she lived
No-one would ever dare
To sit in front of her in church
When she was there at prayer.

And she was always richly dressed
In finest cloth and lace,
She was right handsome in her looks
And very bold of face.

Now she'd been married several times
While she was in her youth,
In fact she'd had five husbands – yes!
I swear this is the truth.

She'd travelled to Jerusalem,
And roamed so far from home,
To Compostella and Boulogne,
She'd even been to Rome.

She had a gap between her teeth,
Encased by fleshy lips,
She wore a flowing mantle that
Concealed her ample hips.

This woman loved to laugh and chat,
She loved to give advice,
About the vagaries of love
She could be quite precise.

After all she'd learnt a lot
On matters of the heart,
And all of this, most cheerfully
She'd willingly impart.

There was a PARSON with us too,
From toil he'd never shirk,
But he was poor – yet wealthy in
All holy thought and work.

He knew the Bible off by heart
And never missed a chance
To preach God's word to one and all –
The Gospel to advance.

He cared for his parishioners
In sickness and in health,
Making no distinction for
The measure of their wealth.

In rain and storm and thunder
He'd go to make a call,
However bad the weather was
Had no effect at all.

And he'd laid out a moral path
On how his flock should live,
It was the best example that
A man of God could give.

'For I'll not run to London town
To earn some dough,' he'd sighed.
'By preaching at the graveside of
Rich folk who have just died.

'No – I will stay here faithfully
With you, my little flock.'
And that's exactly what he did –
As solid as a rock.

His goodness was of finest hue
Which everyone extolled,
And so this loyal man stayed there
And looked out for his fold.

So he was true and virtuous,
Most holy too – but then,
Despite all this he never would
Disparage sinful men.

He'd set a fine example with
His excellent behaviour,
And in this way he hoped to draw
All sinners to their Saviour.

The Parson had a brother who
Had come along with him,
A PLOUGHMAN – he was happy to
Indulge his brother's whim.

This man had moved as many piles
Of heavy, smelly dung
As his dear brother, in his church
Sweet, saintly hymns had sung.

He was an honest working man,
Most handy with a spade,
And lived a life of rectitude
Just as the Bible bade.

He'd dig a ditch and thrash his corn
And live within the law –
For love of Christ he'd do his bit
To help the parish poor.

He paid his taxes right on time
The moment they were due,
He was a really first-class chap,
A good sort through and through.

A MILLER sought to ride with us –
Immense in brawn and bone,
For by his look he must have weighed
Well over sixteen stone.

He liked to boast about his strength,
How he could lift a door
Right off its hinges, o'er his head
Then fling it to the floor.

He had a big, red bushy beard
The colour of a fox,
His balding head displayed a few
Untidy, wispy locks.

Upon his nose there stood right proud
A dark black tuft of hair,
And right beside it I could see
A wart was growing there.

His gaping mouth showed yellow teeth
And from it there would come,
A host of stories, full of filth
That struck most good folk dumb.

And he could tell the quality
Of grain, from just a touch,
And though he knew its proper worth
He'd charge three times as much.

This Miller had some bagpipes too,
Oh, how he loved to play,
And when we left the Tabard Inn,
He piped us on our way.

A MANCIPLE was set to join
Our happy, pious throng,
He'd been resolved for quite a while
That he would come along.

He acted as the caterer
For a special club,
I mean the Inner Temple there –
He purchased all their grub.

He'd watch the markets all the time –
He kept them in his sight,
He'd get in first on any deals
And when the price was right.

Thus he performed his job with care,
He really had a feel
For knowing how to purchase well
And when to strike a deal.

A REEVE was also at the Inn
And he was steward to
A fine estate, yet he had come
To do what Pilgrims do.

He'd taken time to join us all,
To come along and share
Our holy trek to Canterbury
As we all travelled there.

He was an old man – very thin,
Skin tight against the bone,
Short cropped hair and sickly hue –
He travelled all alone.

No auditor could pull the wool
Over his keen eyes,
He could discern within a tick
If he was hearing lies.

For when it came to husbandry
This man was sharp as steel,
A quick look at the weather and
He would declare with zeal,

Just how good the crop would be –
He knew his job all right,
Nothing – not the smallest thing
Escaped this good man's sight.

From just one glance up to the skies
He'd guess the fall of rain,
From this he'd know the quantity
He'd get that year of grain.

His master trusted him and thought
That he could not conceive
He'd ever find a finer man
To be employed as Reeve.

So he was put in charge of all
The pigs and stores and horses,
And tirelessly he took care of
His master's vast resources.

No bailiff, serf or herdsman
Ever tried to pull
Across the eyes of this smart man
The slightest strand of wool.

The Reeve would work out instantly
If someone was a crook,
For he knew every dodgy trick
Contained within life's book.

His master thought he was first-rate
And so it's true to tell
This man had grown quite rich because
His master paid him well.

And so this bent and withered Reeve,
This cranky man, so old,
Now found himself the owner of
A hefty pile of gold.

He rode a stallion-cob who went
By the name of 'Scot',
And this fine horse he'd ride with pride
At firm and steady trot.

They said he hailed from Norfolk,
I'm sure that this was true,
Near a place called Baldeswell
That one or two folk knew.

A SUMMONER had joined us too,
A man whose every thought
Was set on bringing sinners to
The church's sinner's court.

He was filled with saintly zeal,
His eyes, they flashed like fire,
And in his soul a mission burned –
He had but one desire.

To save ungodly sinners –
Turn them from wrong to right,
This man was awful to behold –
A truly fearsome sight.

He frightened children half to death –
Especially little tots,
His eyes were narrow slits, his face
Was covered all in spots.

And every day another batch
Of pimples would appear,
And this poor man tried everything
To get the things to clear.

He liked all alcoholic drinks,
Especially red wine,
And he would drink so much that he
Would generally incline

Towards a bout of shouting – then
He'd yell out crazy things,
It seemed some times that his good sense
Just up and took to wings.

And in our little group there was
A PARDONER as well,
This man had gained permission from
The Pope – for him to sell

Forgiveness and grant pardons –
His one and only goal,
Was to earn a crust of bread –
For cash he'd save your soul.

Now he had only recently
Made his way back home,
For he had been in Italy,
To see the Pope in Rome.

The Pope had given him a stack
Of pardons to hand out,
For cash of course – he wouldn't give
A pardon just for nowt.

He had a weak and silly voice,
His hair was brightest yellow,
His eyes they bulged, his chin was bare,
He was a funny fellow.

But there were two great qualities
This man was famous for,
He preached compelling sermons and
Sang well to any score.

And folk would give their cash to him,
They did it out of choice,
Because they were enraptured by
His fine, melodic voice.

So now you have a good idea
Of all those gathered there,
Secure within the Tabard Inn
And each one set to share

The pilgrimage to Canterbury,
With good, God-fearing heart –
I'll tell you just a little of
The night before our start.

Our HOST there at the Tabard Inn
Bade each to fill a cup
Then raised his glass and told us all
To take our place to sup.

The food he served was excellent,
Tasty and nutritious,
And the wine was quite superb,
Full-bodied and delicious.

As for our Host, he was a man
Of very special worth,
With sparkling eyes and merry laugh
And quite enormous girth,

Which clearly showed to one and all
He loved to wine and dine,
He liked to talk but always knew
Just where to draw the line.

He never said a clumsy thing,
It really was a fact,
This man was always genial
And always full of tact.

Thus when we'd finished eating
He raised his pudgy hand,
And with a smiling countenance
Addressed our merry band.

He said, 'I tell you honestly
In all my happy days
I've never seen a gathering
With such engaging ways.

'And looking at you lovely folk
Has given me a thought,
Something I think that you'll all find
Amusing and great sport.

'You're pilgrims set for Canterbury,
So listen and take heed
To what has just occurred to me
As I bid you "God speed."

'You've many miles to travel,
And countless hours to fill,
Past towns and little villages –
Down dale and then uphill.

'So here's what has occurred to me
To make the time slip by,
A little game that should amuse
And help the hours fly.

'Each one of you should tell a tale
As you journey down
With measured steps and pious hearts
To Canterbury town.

'And when you travel back as well,
Each and everyone
Must make up stories to amuse –
I know it will be fun.

'And then to cap it all – the one
Whose story is the best,
Whose tale gives utmost pleasure and
Stands out above the rest,

'Why, he'll be given such a meal
To celebrate his win,
And it will be when you return –
Right at this very inn.

'He'll have the meal for free, to mark
His story-telling skill,
And he'll not pay a penny as
We all will foot the bill.

'And to ensure fair play, I think
That this is what I'll do,
I'll act as referee and so
Will come along with you.

'That's if you all agree to this,
So shall I be your judge?
And keep you company, as down
To Canterbury you trudge.'

Well, it will come as no surprise,
We readily agreed
That to his judgement we would bow
And willingly would cede.

So glasses were once more filled up,
We drank a grateful toast,
To this fine man, this noble man,
The Tabard Inn's warm Host.

And then to bed, our bellies full,
Our heads awash with wine,
And there we dreamt of Canterbury
And Beckett's holy shrine.

Next morning bright and early
We gathered in a group,
Then with our merry Host set off,
He led our happy troupe.

An hour or two had passed by when
We stopped to quaff a cup,
Our Host then spoke out earnestly,
'Now listen while you sup.

'You all agreed last night we'd tell
Some tales along the way –
So,' said our Host, 'we must decide
Who'll tell a tale today.

'Whoever draws the shortest straw,'
He said with happy grin,
'Shall be the winner, so step up
For then we can begin.'

So each of us then drew a straw,
It was all fairly done,
And everyone was eager now
To see who'd be the one

To start the storytelling,
Who'd be the first to go.
Everybody craned their necks,
Quite eager now to know

On whom would this rare privilege
So deftly now alight.
We all gasped out expectantly
When it became the Knight.

Everyone was cock-a-hoop,
The Knight for his part said,
(Being a man who kept his word
And also nobly bred)

'I gave my word, and freely too,
So as I am to start,
I do so with obedience
And with a willing heart.

'Please listen carefully, my friends
With sympathy, I pray
To this my humble little tale
And all I have to say.'

And so the Knight commenced his tale,
He earnestly began
With not the slightest moment's pause,
And this is how it ran.

And each of them fought viciously
As only suitors can

THE KNIGHT'S TALE

Way back in the past there ruled
A Duke of Athens, who
Went by the name of Theseus –
He was a soldier too.

For he had conquered many lands –
And after one such fight
He met a Queen who dazzled him –
It was true love on sight.

Her name, it was Hippolyta
And they got married there,
Then with her sister Emily,
A girl so sweet and fair,

He set a path to make his way
Back to his Athens home,
Determined now to settle down
And to no longer roam.

But on his way he came across
Some ladies dressed in black.
They cried aloud, they beat their chests,
They called, 'My Lord, Alack!'

You've never seen such sorry sight
None ever could compare
With these poor wretched, grieving souls
Who stood just crying there.

'Whatever is the matter?'
Duke Theseus called out.
'Whatever in the world is this
Lamenting all about?

'Is there something I can do
To put the problem right?
For ladies I have never seen
A more upsetting sight.'

'Have mercy on us,' they all cried
In pitiful distress.
'We crave your help, for we are in
A most appalling mess.

'For we were once fine ladies –
As fine as any seen,
But we've been treated in a way
That's ghastly and obscene.

'For we've lost everything we had,
We who were so grand,
And it was taken from us by
King Creon's filthy hand.

'He is the mighty Lord of Thebes,
His tyranny does fuel
A host of base and awful acts –
Old age has made him cruel.

'Foul Creon killed our husbands – then
He threw them in a pile,
Refusing proper burial rights –
And then this king, so vile

'Set free a pack of hungry dogs –
Let loose from in their pen,
With gnashing jaws and crunching teeth
These dogs devoured our men.

'Oh, my Lord, it is too much,
What we have had to face,
The way King Creon's treated us
Is truly a disgrace!'

The Duke was soft of heart and said,
'This really isn't right.'
And there and then he swore an oath
Like any noble knight

That he would right this awful wrong –
That Creon would now pay
For all his dreadful actions and
He'd make him pay that day.

So Theseus then sent his wife
And her sister too
Ahead to Athens, 'For,' he said,
'There's much I have to do.'

And then he took his army bold
To Thebes, and there he fought,
And very quickly, Thebes' foul king
Was such a lesson taught.

His army was defeated – yes!
His troops all ran away
And Creon, he was slaughtered
By Theseus in the fray.

So Thebes was overwhelmed and then
The mighty Theseus vowed,
'These ladies' husbands now will be
Each wrapped within a shroud.

'And then all proper funeral dues
Must attend their bones
To ease the grieving, aching hearts
Of these poor, broken crones.'

This done, good Theseus took rest –
Within his tent he lay,
And as he did his warriors,
I am most sad to say,

Went pillaging – they robbed the dead
And all the wounded too.
It may seem mean but that is what
The victors used to do.

And in amongst the wounded were
A really sorry pair,
Lying still upon the ground
And almost dying there.

But from the crests upon their chests,
Though spattered all with mud,
They saw at once that these two lads
Were both of royal blood.

They took them to proud Theseus.
He looked them up and down.
'These are great prizes,' he declared,
And then said with a frown,

'We'll take them back to Athens and,
Our prisoners they'll be.
We'll take no ransom for this pair,
They'll never be set free.'

So Theseus went to Athens,
Back to his easy life,
While both the princes were condemned
To a life of strife.

Incarcerated in a cell
Atop a loathsome tower,
And there they tried to while away
Each unforgiving hour.

Year in year out, within this cell
Where they had been installed –
Prince Palamon and Arcite,
As these two lads were called

Did their best to pass the time.
They paced their cell and slept.
But time did not slip by at all,
In truth it only crept.

But then upon one sunny morn
When flowers were in bloom,
Prince Palamon locked in the tower,
Paced up and down the room.

Remembrance of his former life
Seemed far away and hazy,
For life within the tower walls
Was making him go crazy.

He rued the day that he'd been born,
Depressing thoughts ran rife.
This was no way to pass the time,
No way to spend a life.

He cast his eyes from high above
Onto the grounds below,
Upon the lovely morning scene
And Nature's lustrous show.

For it was May and all the world
Was vibrant and alive,
Larks sang, doves cooed, lambs skipped and bees
Were busy in their hive.

The gardens there beneath the tower,
As Palamon looked down,
Were just so lovely that they caused
The poor, jailed prince to frown.

For life in all its grandeur
Was there – but then he saw
An apparition that would change
His life for evermore.

It caused him to gasp out aloud
And then let out a cry,
For his sad eyes had fallen on
A girl as she walked by.

It was the lovely Emily.
She filled him with delight,
And in that moment Cupid's dart
Had swiftly taken flight.

Poor Palamon was now a man
Quite totally possessed,
And from that very moment on
His heart would find no rest.

Arcite, his close cousin asked
When he heard him cry.
'What caused you to call out my friend?
I beg you tell me why.

'You must not let life get you down.
Just learn to let things be.
Accept with resignation that
We'll never be set free.'

Palamon thus answered him,
'My friend, how wrong you are.
I cry because I have just seen
Fair Nature's brightest star.

'A lady whose rare beauty
Would gladden any eye.
It is her loveliness that caused
Your poor cell-mate to cry.

'She surely is a Goddess,'
He gasped with fervent sighs.
'Perhaps she is fair Venus who
Appears here in disguise.'

Arcite then pushed him aside.
He said, 'Let's have a look.'
And in a trice he too was caught
On love's ensnaring hook.

'She must be mine,' he cried aloud.
'Oh, curse this prison cell.'
Thus in a beat he also fell
Prey to the young girl's spell.

Palamon was angry now.
'I saw her first,' he said.
He yelled and remonstrated and
His face went brightest red.

Arcite looked at him with scorn.
He said, 'You thought that she
Was Goddess Venus from on high
So she belongs to me.

'For my love was of human kind
Right from the very first.
I loved her as a woman with
A heart that's fit to burst.

'*Your* love is other worldly,
From somewhere up above,
But mine is of this world and is
A proper kind of love.

'But anyway, why carry on?
Why get worked up and yell?
For we cannot pursue the maid
While locked up in this cell.

'You're wasting all your energy
And it's the same for me,
For Theseus has locked us up
And thrown away the key.'

But still they argued angrily,
And I must sadly tell
There was no longer any peace
In that grim prison cell.

But now our tale moves swiftly on
And we will soon discern
How things then changed and how they took
An unexpected turn.

For Theseus had a visitor,
Perotheus was his name –
The Duke of Athens loved him well,
Perotheus felt the same.

Like any friends they both enjoyed
Each other's company,
And through this friendship, it turned out
Arcite was set free.

Perotheus knew Arcite,
From many years ago,
And when he heard of his sad fate,
Well, he let Theseus know

Just how much he loved the Prince.
He said, 'Please set him free.
I'd take it as a favour if
You'd let him go, for me.'

So Arcite was then released.
'Leave Athens,' Theseus said.
'For if you ever come back here,
You'll be as good as dead.

'Leave this land and don't come back
Or that day you will rue.'
You'd think Arcite would be pleased
But this was not his view.

He sighed, 'I'm so dispirited
That I must now depart,
I truly leave reluctantly
And with a broken heart.

'For now I'll not see Emily
From my prison tower,
Yet Palamon will see her there,
His eyes will still devour

'Her beauty every day, but I
Can only mourn my loss.'
The thought made Arcite morose,
Frustrated and quite cross.

'Palamon has won,' he cried.
'He has come out on top.
If I come back to see my love
Well, I'll be for the chop.

'So go I must, I have no choice.
But what a trial,' he sighed.
'For now without my Emily
I might as well have died.'

Meanwhile, when Palamon was told
That Arcite was freed,
He cried, 'He'll raise an army now
And come back with all speed.

'And he will sack this Athens town,
His army will run rife,
And if he wins he'll quickly make
My Emily his wife.

'And while he then lives happily
With my love by his side,
Within these dank, dark prison walls
This poor prince will reside.'

So this is how young Palamon
Did pass his every day,
While Arcite – back home to Thebes
By then had made his way.

But which one was the saddest?
Well, this is hard to say,
For though a prisoner, Palamon
Saw Emily each day.

Whilst Arcite, though free as air
Could only dream of her.
Which prince's shoes, to wear, would you
I pray, good friend, prefer?

It little matters, you may think,
And that no more befell,
But I would crave your patience for
There is much more to tell.

In Thebes, Arcite had become
A shadow of a man.
He sighed, he groaned, he moped around
As only lovers can.

He couldn't sleep at night – did not
Even take short kips,
And hardly any food or drink
Would ever touch his lips.

He wouldn't speak to anyone.
His love had laid him low,
And even his close family,
He didn't want to know.

People thought he'd gone quite mad.
In some ways this was true.
I'm sure you are familiar
With what deep love can do.

It turns your whole world upside down
And throws you right off course.
Without a doubt the power of love
Is a stupendous force.

And though he suffered for two years
He still remained uncured,
There really was no limit to
The pain the prince endured.

But then one night, when everything
Seemed hopeless and so grim,
Within a dream, winged Mercury,
The god, then came to him.

He spoke in a most certain way,
Said, 'Arcite, dear friend,
You must now go to Athens, where
Your suffering will end.'

The Prince woke up and in a tick
This dream had there performed
A miracle – for Arcite
Was instantly transformed.

No longer pale and wan and grey,
No longer looking sick,
Just one word from Mercury
Had swiftly done the trick.

He stood erect and tall again,
Eyes sparkling, cheeks aglow.
'Right then, that's it,' he cried aloud,
'To Athens I will go.

'And there I'll live dressed in disguise,
And there for life I'll stay,
And then with luck, I'm bound to see
My sweetheart every day.'

And so he made his hopeful way
Back to Athens, where
He got a menial job at court,
But he took every care

To do his work with diligence,
To every task he brought
A willing hand and soon he was
Most valued there at court.

He did some jobs for Emily
So saw a lot of her,
Then Theseus noticed him one day
And started to confer

Great favours onto Arcite
And as he had no notion
Of who he really was, he gave
The young prince a promotion.

Then another, till one day
The mighty Theseus swore,
'Upon my soul, there really is
No man I value more.'

So now we see that Arcite
Is really doing well
Our thoughts should turn to Palamon
So that I may here tell

Of his sad fate, his awful life
Within that jail so grim,
For I should surely let you know
What has befallen him.

Well, he has languished in his cell
Year after awful year
With no-one to show sympathy
Or help him out, I fear.

But then when seven years had passed
The prince received some aid
To help him break his chains and thus
A bold escape was made.

A friend had come to help him flee,
He'd used the strongest drink
To knock the jailer out and then
From that foreboding clink

Young Palamon at last escaped,
He ran into the night
To seek a secret place to hide
For it would soon be light.

And then he worked out what he'd do
'I'll go to Thebes,' he thought.
'For it is time a lesson should
To Theseus now be taught.

'I'll raise an army, then return,
I'll conquer Athens town,
And then make Emily my wife
And she will wear my crown.

'But for the moment I must wait
Till it is safe to go.'
He hid deep in a bush, and thought,
'It's best if I lay low.'

And that is where we'll leave the prince,
Outside of Athens town,
Hiding tensely in a bush,
And with his head well down.

So back now to young Arcite
Who has become a Squire,
Close servant to great Theseus
Thus dressed in grand attire.

Life is good – up to a point
But passions still run rife,
For still he hopes that one day, he'll
Make Emily his wife.

But now he has some time to spare
And he decides to ride
Out to the country, near the spot
Where Palamon does hide.

He rides awhile and then dismounts
And says with measured sigh,
'I'll rest right here' – he doesn't know
His old friend hides close by.

He sat down on the lush, green grass,
Head resting on his hand,
And glumly there he reminisced
About his distant land.

'To think that I, a prince of Thebes
Should end up in this mire,
Here in Athens, working as
An evil tyrant's Squire.

'To end up being servant to
My greatest foe like this,
Could be transformed to ecstasy,
Could easily be bliss,

'If only dearest Emily
Would spare me just one look.'
And as he spoke of his dear love
His every fibre shook.

Emotions wracked his very soul,
His passions were on fire,
He cried, 'In this world, Emily,
You're all that I desire.'

Now hiding in the bush close by
Palamon heard him speak.
He thought, 'That's my dear Emily
Of whom he speaks, what cheek!'

So leaping from the bush he cried,
'Arcite, I am here,
And your base words have now assured
That you have much to fear.

'How dare you love my Emily,
And though I have no sword,
Still will I fight till one of us
Lies dead upon this sward.'

Arcite saw his cousin there
And said with great disdain,
'I never ever thought I'd see
Your stupid face again.

'I'd kill you now without a thought
If you were not unarmed,
But as you have no weaponry
You can leave here unharmed.

'But pray come back tomorrow
And I will bring with me
Weapons for us both and then
We will surely see

'Just how brave you really are,
We'll fight till our last breath,
Although I guarantee 'twill be
You cousin – who meets death.'

And so on this they both agreed –
What a scene of sorrow,
That these two who had been such friends
Would fight upon the morrow.

Next day the two young princes met,
They stood there face to face.
Arcite said, 'There's armour here,
A shield, a sword, a mace.'

They helped each other don their suits
But neither said a word,
No kindly salutation in
That verdant glade was heard.

And once they were quite fully armed
Well, then the fight began,
And each of them fought viciously
As only suitors can.

For only those who love, will fight
With such ferocious zeal
And demonstrate unflinchingly
That they have nerves of steel.

Both Palamon and Arcite
Tried everything to be
The victor so that they could claim
The love of Emily.

They struck each other ruthlessly
Exchanging blow for blow,
And as they fought they opened wounds
And blood began to flow.

It very rapidly became
A stream and then a flood,
And in but little time the ground
Was slippery with blood.

Sword crashed on sword relentlessly
And yet they battled still,
They both fought on with bravery
And quite outstanding skill.

The contest would have carried on
And on and on and on,
Till it grew late, until indeed
The sun no longer shone.

But then who should pass by that way
But Theseus – by chance
And he demanded, 'What's all this?'
As he looked on askance.

He was out hunting with his court
In that wood, lush and green,
Fair Emily was with him too
As was his wife, the queen.

When he espied the duelling pair
His anger boiled and then,
He cried, 'Desist from fighting now,
You disrespectful men.

'How dare you fight within my wood,
And with no umpire here,
Desist right now or in a trice
I'll split you ear to ear.

'What is the reason that you fight
With such ferocity?
The hatred in your hearts is clear
For everyone to see.'

Well, Palamon, he spoke up first,
'My Lord, you may ask why
We fight, but I must say in truth
We both deserve to die.

'For there before you stands the man
Who served you as your Squire.
The one who carried out, my Lord
Your every last desire.

'But I tell you, he played you false
For he's no other than
Prince Arcite, on whom, my Lord
You did impose a ban.

'You said that if he ever came
To Athens – then he'd die,
But he came back and in disguise,
And now I'll tell you why.

'He has the sheer effrontery
To love dear Emily,
Even though that gracious girl
By right, belongs to me.

'For I am Palamon, who broke
So boldly from your jail,
And I stand here with little hope,
For it's to no avail,

'To plead for mercy, as I know
I'd surely waste my breath,
So I ask but this one small thing –
Arcite too meets death,

'For both of us deserve to die,
For both of us each hate
The other with a vengeance, so
Should share the self-same fate.'

Theseus looked upon the pair
And then said, 'I agree.
You've been condemned by your own hand
And so that's what will be.

'You've asked for death and this I'll grant,
One that is swift and sure,
Enacted fairly and upheld
By our Athenian law.'

Now when the Queen heard Theseus speak,
Well, she began to cry,
And said in her soft-heartedness
The princes should not die.

She said that surely their one sin
From everything she'd seen
Was nothing more than they had loved –
To kill them would be mean.

A passionate and loving heart
Was really way above
All other feelings, for it was
A sacred thing to love.

And as she spoke, fair Emily
Also grew most fraught,
And it took but a moment till
The females of the court

All joined in tearful remonstrance,
They begged great Theseus there
To spare the princes from the axe
And let them show them care,

For all the ladies there had seen
With tearful, red-rimmed eyes,
The princes' wounds, and this had caused
Their pleading and their cries.

Theseus looked upon his queen
And ladies of the court,
And being kind of heart he then
Granted what they sought.

For he had thought unto himself,
'It's natural, after all
For young men to pursue their heart
And answer to love's call.

'And any man locked up in jail
Would try to break away,
Only a fool, with a half a chance
Would ever choose to stay.'

So as he stood reflecting there
His heart began to melt,
Till slowly, then with more resolve
He changed the way he felt.

He said, 'These royal princes here
Had every chance to fly,
But chose to stay and for their love
They were prepared to die.

'Oh, what a fool a man becomes
When love ensnares his heart,
It makes all thought and common sense
And fear for self depart.

'And yes, I also know, full well
What fervent love can do,
For in my time I've also been
A lover like these two.

'It pulls a man this way and that
And causes him such pain
That truthfully he never thinks
That he'll be sane again.

'And as I too have been ensnared
I will forgive you both,
But in return I do insist
That you now take an oath,

'That you will never rage against
My Athens any more,
Or bring an army to these lands
Intent on waging war.'

The princes there and then pronounced
On oath, that they'd agree,
So Theseus said they were his friends,
And let them both go free.

'But what about dear Emily
Whom both of you adore?
For anything she does must be
Within the bounds of law.

'And she can't marry both of you
As everybody knows,
And so dear princes, this is what
I formally propose.

'In one year's time, you shall return.
Come to this very place,
And each must bring a hundred knights
And be prepared to face

'The other side, there in the lists –
Whoever proves to be
The greater fighter, bolder knight,
Well, he'll wed Emily.'

Palamon, he jumped for joy
And said, 'I'll gladly fight.'
And Arcite, he punched the air
To show his great delight.

And so the princes galloped off,
Left Athens in their rear.
But each was quite determined that
He would return next year,

To fight the other prince – and win
The hand of Emily,
And do it in the name of love
And knightly chivalry.

A year passed by and Theseus
Did lavishly engage
Artists and artisans to make
A massive, sweeping stage

On which the noble pair would fight –
The lists were quite unique,
A truly stunning stage on which
The princes would now seek

A victory to win the hand
Of her whom they adored.
Only one like Theseus
Could such a scene afford.

What lavishness and opulence
Were brashly on display
It was the kind of tapestry
That took your breath away.

For paintings hung on every wall
And statues did abound
Around the lists – fine art soon filled
Each unused piece of ground.

When all was done, it was surveyed
From each and every side
By Theseus, who was well pleased,
'It's wonderful,' he sighed.

But now the time at last arrived
For matters to commence,
You've never felt an atmosphere
Alive with such suspense.

The whole of Athens waited with
Expectant, baited breath
For they all knew they had in store
A battle to the death.

Then finally the princes came,
Two noble, gallant knights
Each set to win fair Emily
And put his life to rights.

They rode into the lists – a sight
To thrill the stalest mind
And stir up even those who weren't
Pugnaciously inclined.

Bedecked in heavy armour,
The princes grinned and waved,
The Athens' crowd, they shouted out,
Hysterically they raved.

Behind each prince – a spectacle –
The most amazing sights,
With banners flying, swords aloft –
There rode a hundred knights.

And many in the crowd there said
That not in time before
Had any seen such worthy knights,
And many even swore

That there had never, ever been
In God's world far and wide
A scene so great and glorious,
Just there to win a bride.

Then Theseus raised his hand and spoke,
He cried above the din.
He said, 'These princes both must rest,
No fighting will begin

'Until they have refreshed themselves
And had fine wine and food,
And made their peace with God – and then
We'll settle this old feud.'

And he was true unto his word,
He laid on such a spread
That made quite sure that everyone
Was amply wined and fed.

And all of Athens readily
Agreed there'd never been
Such feasting in the realm before –
The best they'd ever seen.

The night before the princes' duel,
Before the break of day,
Palamon heard a lark – it sang
In quite the strangest way.

It woke him from his slumber – and
In quiet, solemn mood,
With pious heart and head bowed down,
And thinking of the feud,

He made his way with measured tread,
Through the morning mists,
Unto a temple, built upon
A spot close to the lists.

And kneeling then in piety
He mouthed a fervent prayer.
A solitary, humble man
Just begging mercy there.

He whispered, 'If it is your will
To grant me victory,
Then so be it – but if 'tis not,
Then so shall matters be.

'If Arcite should come out best
And take this sinner's life,
As I'll be dead, I'll care not that
He makes my love his wife.

'But what I hope and wish so much,
The object of my prayer,
Is that I win fair Emily
And take her in my care.

'To be my dear companion
Through the trials of life,
To be a loving, faithful spouse,
A loyal, pious wife.'

And as he prayed, sweet Emily
Was saying her prayers too,
And she was so confused for she
Did not know what to do.

Who should she love? Which one was best?
It was so hard to tell.
In truth both princes in their way
Had cast a magic spell.

Yet it would be desirable
If only they would see
That loving her brought agony.
She cried, 'Oh, turn from me!

'And drown your love, put out the fires
That make your passions rage.
Oh princes both, desist from this
And do not take the stage.

'Do not fight and spill your blood
In the lists tomorrow.
Your actions will just cause more hate
And quite appalling sorrow.'

But then she looked up wistfully,
Her cheeks aglow, like fire,
'But if fair princes, fight you must,
Then it is my desire,

'That he who comes out conqueror,
He who wins the day,
Will be the prince who in his heart
Can claim and truly say,

'That he loved me the most – that he
Adored me way above
The other prince and won because
The greater was his love.'

꧁꧂

We'll leave fair Emily at prayer –
Go to another place,
To where Arcite prays for strength,
His grave ordeal to face.

He cried, 'Oh Lord, I know I'm weak,
My suffering is long,
But with your help my pain will ease
And you will make me strong.

'So on the morrow, this I pray,
With passion – to you Lord,
Give strength and vigour to my arm
And power to my sword.

'And grant me then a victory
That I can then entwine
My life with fairest Emily
And make the sweet girl mine.'

And so the scene had now been set
The day had come at last
When all would be resolved – and yes
The die would soon be cast.

And what a day it was that dawned,
For spring had just then sprung.
It was the merry month of May,
A great time to be young.

The town was filled with chattering,
Excitement filled the air
For everyone was keen to see
Just how the lads would fare.

The knights prepared their horses,
Their harnesses pulled tight,
And every heart there beat with pride
Determined now to fight.

It was a scene of bustle,
Of urgency and all.
Each man was nervous and pent up
At what might now befall.

And then Duke Theseus appeared,
The crowd all strained to hear
What he would say, heed his commands –
So everyone drew near.

He said, 'It is my dearest wish
To change the rules – for I
Would much prefer that all should live,
That no-one here should die.

'And so I here and now decree
No cross-bows can be used
Or stabbing swords and I insist
These rules are not abused.

'And every man will be confined
To running but one course,
And if he's injured with a lance
Or thrown from off his horse,

'Well then he'll be conveyed with speed
To safety, there to rest
Content within the knowledge that
He fought and did his best.

'Combatants all, may use a mace
Or wield a long broadsword.'
And every knight on hearing this
Assented to the Lord.

And then he said and sadly too,
'If in this fearsome brawl
Either prince should take a wound
And to the ground then fall,

'Or be dragged off unwillingly
By overpowering force,
Unto a stake placed in the ground –
Then if things take this course,

'We will proclaim that he has lost.
The other wins the day.
And now I have but one last word
That I would wish to say.

'If one brave prince be killed outright,
All fighting we'll suspend,
And we'll declare that this dispute
Is over – at an end.'

Then Theseus sat down between
His Queen and Emily,
He clasped his hands and calmly said,
'So now it's time to see

'The worth of these two princes –
Which one will prove to be
A proper suitor then a spouse
For sister Emily.'

He waved his hand and from above
A herald loudly cried,
'This is the time bold knights to prove,
With honour and with pride,

'Your manliness upon this field,
Prepare yourselves and then
Come forth to fight with chivalry –
Equip yourselves as men.'

Well, what a battle now ensued,
Lance crashed upon a shield,
Sword clashed on sword and mace on mace,
And neither side would yield.

Those sitting in the crowd could hear
The awful, dreadful tones
Of crying men of crashing swords,
The crunching of cracked bones.

The knights fought on remorselessly,
Ankle deep in mud,
The crowd were mesmerised to see
Great spouts of gushing blood.

Horses reared and tumbled too,
Their bright eyes flashed with fear.
They fell on knights who didn't have
The time to stumble clear.

Then in the midst of battle,
In all the gore and heat,
Our two young princes finally
With eagerness, now meet.

This is the final reckoning
Of their on-going war,
To put an end to all their fights
And settle their old score.

They fought, spurred on with jealousy
And overpowering hate.
Still full of vigour, even though
The hour was growing late.

Exchanging awful, savage blows,
Some dreadful wounds each took,
But giving up was not a choice
That either prince would brook.

But then a knight there intervened,
He thrust his sword into
The side of Palamon – it was
An unfair thing to do.

But don't they say that all is fair
In love and yes, in war.
Poor Palamon was weakened now
And could resist no more.

Twenty men then dragged the prince
To the loser's stake.
He lay there breathing heavily
And thought his heart would break.

For in that moment it was clear
That his long fight was done.
That he was vanquished and his foe
Bold Arcite had won.

When Theseus saw this happen –
Saw Palamon dragged to
The stake – he knew there surely was
But one thing left to do.

He cried aloud, 'Stop everything
And let us now seek peace.
Lay down your arms for I insist
All fighting now must cease.'

The crowd fell silent at the sight
Of Theseus, so grand.
He then decreed, 'Young Arcite
Shall take my sister's hand,

'For he has conquered, fair and square.
Oh, what a win this is.
He did it by the jousting rules.
The victory is his'

Well, how the crowd went crazy then –
No-one there disputed
This result – they all cried out
And hollered, cheered and hooted.

Hats were thrown into the air
And trumpeters blared out.
This was a very special day,
Of this, no-one could doubt.

Arcite's heart was bursting now.
Oh, what a day for him.
But wait a while, for Fortune can
Turn on a fickle whim.

When all is won it can be lost.
That's just the way of things.
And Fortune can make fools of all,
From peasants through to kings.

So now we see brave Arcite
Ride his charger round
The great arena – which vibrates
With a cheering sound.

The yelling and the shouting rise
To one almighty roar.
All thoughts are gone of gushing blood,
And wounds and death and gore.

For every eye within that place
Just falls upon one man,
On Arcite – who rides around
As only heroes can.

With sword aloft and head held high,
He greeted everyone,
And to a man they feted him
For everything he'd done.

His eyes then fell on Emily,
And she too, for her part,
Returned his gaze most willingly
To show he'd won her heart.

For now that he had won the fight
She was most happy to
Confirm she loved him and to state
She'd always held that view.

The ladies like a winner
And it is true to say
That Emily loved Arcite
Now he had won the day.

So in triumph, Arcite
So upright, bold and proud
Rode with a victor's haughtiness
And waved to that great crowd.

But then a mighty gasp went up,
For Arcite's fine horse
Took fright and threw the bold, young prince,
With an almighty force,

Out from his saddle, to the ground;
He fell and hit his head.
To everybody looking on
It seemed the prince was dead.

They carried him with every care,
For he was breathing still,
Unto a great physician who
Was famous for his skill.

He nursed Arcite but proclaimed,
'Though I intend to give
This brave young knight kind nurturing,
I still don't think he'll live.'

Arcite's health went up and down.
Some days he was okay.
But other times he quite relapsed –
And then one mournful day,

His lungs collapsed, his face turned grey
And it was very clear
To everyone who looked at him,
That death was drawing near.

He cried, 'Please send for Emily,
For I must say goodbye,
And hold her in my poor, weak arms
Once more, before I die.'

She came with haste unto his side.
He gasped, 'Draw close to me,
For from now on – within my grave
I'll have no company.

'So take me in your arms, my love.
And let me feel your touch.
Farewell my darling Emily,
For you, I bore so much.'

And then he said, 'If ever now
You choose to be a wife,
Dear Palamon would make a fine
Companion for life.'

And then the numbing fingers of
Cold death began to creep
Across his body, but it seemed
That he lay there asleep.

He slowly opened listless eyes –
But found he couldn't see,
And then he uttered these last words,
'Oh mercy ... Emily.'

And then this noble prince gasped out
And Emily, she cried,
And as she sobbed and cast around
The doomed Arcite died.

Poor Emily, she was distraught,
So awful was her pain.
She couldn't bear to think that she
Would not see him again.

And Palamon was borne down too
With overpowering sorrow.
It was as if the world would end,
That there'd be no tomorrow.

Then Theseus, with sadness said,
'We must now find a plot,
On which to build a monument –
A very special spot,

'To recognise great Arcite,
His bravery and grace.
Somewhere to honour him with pride
A cherished, stately place.'

And then the Duke of Athens had
A really touching thought,
To build it in the glade wherein
The princes first had fought.

And so they fashioned it and took
Arcite on a bier
To the glade and placed with him
A shield, a sword and spear.

And then they set the prince alight
Upon a funeral pyre.
And his cold body burnt to ash
In all consuming fire.

When later things had settled down
Duke Theseus then brought
His much loved sister Emily
And Palamon to court.

He said, 'You both have known great loss.
Such sorrow you have borne,
And I know for lost Arcite
The pair of you still mourn.

'But from two sorrows can't we now
Apply this simple ploy,
And join them both to then create
One certain, perfect joy?

'For sister dear, this gentle knight,
So full of noble grace,
Has loved you with a steady will
Since first he saw your face.

'He is the nephew of a king.
A worthy prince,' he said.
'And therefore he's most suitable
For you, my dear, to wed.'

And so it was that Palamon,
After years of strife
Took Emily to be his own
Beloved, faithful wife.

And they lived happily for years
And no-one ever heard
An argument between them or
A harsh or angry word.

And so this is the story
Of fairest Emily
And Palamon – and then our Knight
Looked at the company,

A smile upon his face he said,
'Here ends my tale,' and then
He bowed to all of us and sighed,
'That's it my friends – Amen.'

He said astride his poor, old horse,
In truth, half-on, half-off

THE MILLER'S PROLOGUE

Well, everyone had listened to
The tale, told deftly by
The Knight, and all agreed it was
A tale to make you sigh.

For it was sad, but what a twist
At the very end,
A noble tale, one of the best
Ever to be penned.

Our Host laughed out and gaily cried,
'As far as I can tell
We've started really admirably,
It's going very well.

'So who will now take to the floor
And merrily regale
Our band of faithful pilgrims here,
With yet another tale?

'Who'll accept the challenge?
What say you Sir Monk?'
But then up spoke the Miller who
Was sadly very drunk.

He sat astride his poor, old horse,
In truth, half-on, half-off,
And merrily, a glass of ale
The Miller there did quaff.

Our Host could see immediately
From how his shoulders slunk
That the Miller was half gone,
All bleary-eyed and drunk.

'Hold on good fellow,' he replied,
'Hold a tick, dear brother.
I think it might be better if
We heard now from another.'

'Upon my soul,' the Miller cried,
'I mean to have my way,
I've got a worthy story here
And I *will* have my say.'

Our Host gave up and said, 'Okay.
You fool! You silly bore!
For as you are so very drunk
You'll mess it up for sure.'

The Miller laughed and said, 'If I
Get mixed up in my tale,
Then put it down to just the fact
I've supped too much good ale.'

And so he told his tale to us,
With warts and all, it's this,
And I apologise if you
Find some of it amiss.

He lay there with his eyes fast shut,
His mouth was open wide

THE MILLER'S TALE

A carpenter from Oxford town
Had a thought one day,
To make some extra cash – he'd have
A lodger in to stay.

'It will help me pay the bills,'
The carpenter had said.
'He'll only need a modest room
In which to lay his head.'

And so he advertised and found
A likely looking lad
Who'd been searching round the town
To find himself a pad.

This youth was known as Nicholas
And he was famous for
Predicting what the future held,
What it would have in store.

He'd studied in geometry –
Astrology as well,
So everybody thought that he
Could accurately foretell

Just what the fickle fates would bring,
What would happen next.
It seemed he could predict for sure
On life's unwritten text.

A deal was struck, the young man said,
'It's comfortable, it's fine.
I'll soon create a home right here
And make this room feel mine.'

And that's exactly what he did,
He placed in all the nooks
His fragrant herbs, his harp, his fruit
And all his many books.

He'd often play his harp and sing
To all the folk who came,
And they'd reward him with applause
And rapturous acclaim.

And thus he spent his time and plucked
Tunes on his harp and then
He'd tell the fortunes of the folk
And what would happen when.

Now though the carpenter was old –
Had seen a lot of life,
He'd decided recently
To wed a brand new wife.

Don't ask me how he did it
But this old reprobate
Had got a girl of eighteen years
To be his life-long mate.

And it will come as no surprise
For you to learn, that he
Was really quite as jealous as
A man could ever be.

He should have wed another wife.
Someone not so young.
Someone closer to his age
And not so highly strung.

For she was young and wild and game
For any youthful lark,
While he was old and had long since
Lost his impulsive spark.

She had an hourglass figure
And flowing, flaxen hair,
Ruby lips and flashing eyes
And skin so smooth and fair.

She was a sight to make a man
Draw in his breath and sigh,
She was in truth a gorgeous girl,
A feast for any eye.

Then one day her husband said,
'I'll be away today.
I have some business to sort out
Close down by Osney way.'

Once he had gone, young Nicholas
Came sneaking from his room,
And there he found the lovely girl
All busy with her broom.

Now Nicholas was flesh and blood
And he could not resist
Her charm – so on this day he caught
The young girl by her wrist.

He twirled her round in playful mood
And made her skip and jump,
And then most cheekily he placed
His hand upon her rump.

He cried, 'Unless I have you now
I swear to you I'll die.'
He squeezed her cheek and caused the girl
To gasp out loud and cry.

She jumped away and said to him,
'I won't! Now let me go!
If you do not desist, I'll shout
And let the neighbours know.'

But Nicholas would not give up,
He dropped onto his knees,
And then with flowery, scholar's words,
And such heart-rending pleas

He told her of his love for her
Which nothing could e'er quench –
And then in time a smile did cross
The face of this wild wench.

She said, 'All right – I'll find a way.
But we must both beware.
My husband is a jealous man
And so we must take care.

'If he finds out I've been untrue,
'Twill mean my certain death.'
Nicholas, with gleaming eye
Replied, with catch of breath,

'Don't give a thought to that old fool.
(Raw lust was now his spur.)
A scholar does not need much wit
To trick a carpenter.'

So they reached an understanding
That they would find a way
To consummate their lustful thoughts
Upon some future day.

But before the young lad left
He fondled her a bit,
Then played his harp – and thus the fires
Of love and lust were lit.

And then one day this fickle wife
Made her way to church
To make amends and set herself
Back on her pious perch.

And as she prayed and did those things
God-fearing women do,
She came within the gaze of one
Who vowed he loved her too.

This was the parish clerk, whose name
Was Absolon and he
Would sigh and groan when she was near
And cry, 'She tortures me.'

Everything about the lass
Set his poor heart awhirl,
He was completely overcome
And smitten by the girl.

And so one evening he repaired
Unto the young girl's house.
Now you'd have thought on reaching it
He'd move just like a mouse.

Silently – and with great stealth
So no-one saw him there.
But no – he stood for all to see
And sang without a care.

His voice was full of passion.
Sweet words of love he sang.
And in the bedroom up above
His singing boldly rang.

It caused the carpenter to wake.
He shouted out, 'By 'eck.
Do you hear that fool Absolon?
I should go ring his neck.

'Alison, d'you hear?' he cried.
'What Absolon is doing.
He's down there and it is to you
That he directs his wooing.'

'Yes, dear John,' the wife replied.
'I hear the fool all right.'
And that is all she said to him
Except to say, 'Goodnight!'

But Absolon was undeterred,
He kept his wooing going
To show his love for Alison –
He had no way of knowing

That she loved sneaky Nicholas,
That scholar in his prime.
So lovelorn Absolon in truth
Did surely waste his time.

However much he sang his songs
Or over her did drool,
It cut no ice with Alison
She thought him but a fool.

But then there came a Saturday
When the carpenter
Went off to see a friend with whom
He needed to confer.

Once he was gone, young Nicholas
And Alison agreed
To put a crafty plan in place
And do it with all speed.

For they were both resolved and keen
To do what e'er they might
To have a loving rendezvous,
Together and all night.

They planned to lead the carpenter
A right old merry dance,
And make him think that Nicholas
While in a holy trance

Had had a premonition
Of things that were to come –
'Twould all be false, a sneaky plan
To which he would succumb.

So Nicholas took to his room
Enough to drink and eat
To last a day or two – he had
Strong ale, some bread and meat.

He'd hide away and Alison
Would tell her spouse, old John
On his return – she'd no idea
Where Nicholas had gone.

So when old John came back she said,
'We've no idea at all
Where Nicholas has gone, for he
Seems not to heed our call.'

Saturday passed – and Sunday came
And still there was no sign
Of Nicholas – and thus word spread
On Oxford's swift grapevine

That maybe he'd gone off and died –
The carpenter then said,
'I fear for poor, young Nicholas.
I think he may be dead.'

And then he told his servant-boy,
'Though it may prove in vain,
Get up those stairs and shout out loud
And kick his door again,

'For maybe Nicholas is there,
Sick and all alone.
So bash the door with all your force
And use a staff or stone.'

So up the servant-boy then goes.
'Hey Nicholas,' he cries.
'Don't stay abed all day like this,
It's lazy and unwise.

'It's bad for health.' and then he used
A very naughty word.
This made no difference – from the room
No single sound was heard.

But then the servant-boy looked down
And saw there in the wall
A hole through which the old black cat
Was often wont to crawl.

So he lay down and looked right through,
Then quaked with fearful dread.
For there he saw young Nicholas
Flat out upon the bed.

He lay there on his back, his mouth
Was open wide, his eyes
Stared at the ceiling, so it seemed
Quite fair thus to surmise,

That Nicholas could be stone dead
Or in some awful trance.
Could he be saved, brought back to life?
There seemed but little chance.

The boy rushed to the carpenter
And told what he had seen.
Old John was certain that he knew
What this strange thing did mean.

'His messing with astronomy
Has sent him off his head,
Or even worse, it's killed the lad.
It looks as if he's dead.

'Go get a staff, we'll force the door
And if he lives, I swear
I'll shake this nonsense out of him,
So he will need beware,

'For I'll not have him doing this –
Messing with this stuff.
I tell you all and honestly
I've really had enough.'

And so they brought a staff and forced
The heavy bedroom door,
And as they did old John there puffed,
Blasphemed and cursed and swore.

When finally the door caved in,
Old John then strode inside.
He cried out, 'Wake up, Nicholas,
This stuff I'll not abide.'

He shook the lad most vigorously
And Nicholas came round.
He lay there on the bed – at first
He stared and made no sound.

Then breathing heavily he sighed,
'Must this sweet world now end?'
Then turning to old John he said,
'Bring me some liquor, friend.

'And once I've drunk, I do intend
In secret, then to tell
Of things affecting you and me –
And you must listen well.

'And never tell another soul
Of what I do impart,
But first of all bring me some ale
And then I'll make a start.'

The carpenter obeyed at once,
A jug of ale was brought,
They shut the door and Nicholas
Commenced his naughty sport.

He said, 'Now dear old John, sweet friend
You never must betray
A single word of what I now
Intend to say today.

'For I impart our Saviour's word
And if you ever tell,
Well, you'll be driven crazy and
Reserve your place in hell.'

That stupid fool, that silly John,
That man so quite absurd
Replied, 'I promise faithfully
I'll never breathe a word.'

So Nicholas began his tale.
He said, 'Astrology
Has shown the future clearly now,
So listen carefully.

'Next Monday night such rains will come
Resembling Noah's flood.
Great torrents of wild, crashing foam
And everywhere black mud.

'The world will disappear beneath
This flood – such loss of life.'
Old John cried out, 'What will become
Of my sweet, darling wife?

'Is she to die? Oh tell me no.
This is too much to bear.
Is there no remedy?' – Poor John
Was borne down with despair.

Crafty Nicholas then spoke.
'Don't get into a tizz.
With help from our dear, precious Lord,
I tell you that there is.

'For he helps those who help themselves,
So here is what we'll do,
You must fetch three ample tubs,
For me, your wife and you.

'And when the mighty waters come,
Well, in the tubs we'll hide
And bounce upon the waters till
They finally subside.

'So take them to the barn and put
Provisions in each one
So we will have some nourishment
Once the flood's begun.

'Now hurry off and do all this.
Don't tell another soul.
For this to work, great secrecy
Must be our earnest goal.

'And John, you must no longer seek
With lustful looks and pleas
A closeness with your wife – for this
Is what the Lord decrees.'

And so the naive carpenter
Rushed off within a tick
To get the tubs and set them up.
The poor chap was just thick.

For then he went to see his wife
And told her all he knew,
And she pretended to be scared
Which we know was untrue.

For she was in the know and knew
Of Nicholas' plan.
This scheming wife was making fun
Of this poor silly man.

When all these tasks had been achieved.
Victuals stored, tubs ready,
Nicholas declared, 'Hold fast.
Stay resolute, be steady.'

And then when Monday night arrived
He told the other two,
'Let's go now to the barn – prepare
To see this great flood through.'

So off they went and settled down
And they began to pray,
That the Lord would get them through
This very dangerous day.

Old John then climbed into a tub
Slung just above the floor,
And in a tick he fell asleep
And soon began to snore.

He lay there with his eyes fast shut,
His mouth was open wide,
And Nicholas and Alison
Sat watching by his side.

'Is he asleep?' breathed Alison.
'Dead to the world,' he said.
So with no further word, the pair
Soon made their way to bed.

They left the barn and sleeping John,
Elated that they'd won,
For now they'd have their wicked way,
At last they'd have their fun.

On the very self-same day
That our old friend, poor John
Had been the victim of this gross
And quite outrageous con,

The parish clerk, young Absolon
Had gone that very day
To visit some good friends of his
Who lived not far away.

And there in conversation
He said, 'I haven't seen
Old John, the carpenter around.
Wherever has he been?'

One man replied, ' I think he's gone
To fetch some timber for
The Abbot – and he'll be away
A day or even more.'

Well, Absolon on hearing this
Sat upright with a start,
His hand was shaking – in his breast
He felt his pounding heart.

'The carpenter's away,' he thought.
'Oh, this is really great,
I'll go and woo dear Alison
And maybe get a date.

'I'll to her bedroom window
And tap on it tonight,
And tell her of my love and then
With luck, this will ignite

'A love for me within her heart.
Oh yes and then what bliss,
For I am sure she'll favour me
At least with one sweet kiss.'

And so that night young Absolon
Went off and tapped upon
The bedroom window of his love –
Old John's wife, Alison.

He called in honeyed tones and all.
He called her 'little bird'.
And Alison abed inside
Heard each and every word.

She heard him call her 'sweetheart dear'.
And 'dearest honey dove'.
And how he swore with certainty
She was his only love.

Of course – right at that moment
She was ensconced within,
Wrapped in the arms of Nicholas
Committing carnal sin.

And so she cried, 'Clear off, you fool.'
He called, 'You are my belle.'
To which she answered caustically,
'You can go to hell.

'I love another, Absolon,
So go away,' she cried.
Poor Absolon on hearing this
Felt as though he'd died.

It is the way of this cruel world
But then she heard him say,
'Grant me but one sweet, loving kiss
And I'll be on my way.'

Alison replied and said,
'And if I do – you'll go?'
And Absolon assured her thus,
'One kiss and 'twill be so.'

So out of bed leapt Alison.
She said, 'That stupid lout.
Leave this to me dear Nicholas,
I'll sort this whole thing out.'

The night was black as sooty coal.
You couldn't see a thing,
When Alison with nothing on
Thus from her bed did spring.

Nicholas, in bed, laughed out
While she, as bold as brass
Strode to the window shamelessly
And there poked out her arse.

She said, 'So take just one sweet kiss.
Then Absolon, depart.'
He cried aloud, 'I will my dear
With all my loving heart.'

And so he puckered up his lips
To take the proffered crumb,
And then he planted a huge kiss
On her protruding bum.

But as he kissed it he began
To think 'something's amiss.
This is a most unusual
And funny kind of kiss.'

And then sweet Alison withdrew,
She pulled herself inside.
Then Nicholas began to laugh
So much he almost cried.

He laughed (and Absolon did hear).
'Oh that crass, stupid bloke.
He kissed your arse, oh Alison,
That's what I call a joke.'

When Absolon heard Nicholas
Mock him in this way
He vowed in anger and in shame,
'I swear I'll make them pay.'

In but an instant, love had gone,
It flew right out the door.
His ardour for sweet Alison
Had died and lived no more.

The kissing of her nether parts
Had now quite turned his mood.
He thought the joke was in bad taste,
Unfunny and quite rude.

And so he vowed to take revenge,
Right there and straightaway,
He wouldn't waste a moment now –
He would not brook delay.

He went to see the smith, Gervase.
His face was angry red.
'Will you lend me a branding iron?'
Galled Absolon then said.

The blacksmith said, 'No problem son.'
And gave him one, red hot.
'This will leave its mark – you'll see
When placed on any spot.'

So back went Absolon well armed
With the steaming iron.
He gnashed his teeth and growled aloud
Just like an angry lion.

He tapped upon the window there
And called, 'My precious thing,
Dear Alison – it's Absolon
And I've brought you a ring.'

Nicholas, within the room
Heard the lover's cry
And thought, 'That fool is here again
To have another try.

'Well – I believe I can improve
On what we did before.'
He little knew what Absolon,
Outside, now had in store.

The bedroom window, he unlatched
And flung it open wide.
Then in the dark he hung his rear
Quite fearlessly outside.

As Absolon then cried out loud,
'My precious, dear sweet-heart.'
That naughty Nicholas let fly
The most enormous fart.

Absolon was not deterred.
He held the iron tight,
And then he thrust it upwards with
His every ounce of might.

There came the most tremendous cry
And such a smell of frying,
Poor Nicholas, who leapt with pain
Thought he, for sure, was dying.

In agony he cried out loud,
'Oh water, please pour some,
Oh Alison, for heavens sake
Pour water on my bum.'

Meanwhile, close by, the carpenter
Just lying in a heap
Was woken by poor Nicholas
From his deep, fitful sleep.

He heard his cries for water.
They really chilled his blood.
He thought, 'Oh Gawd! Lord help us,
For here comes Noah's flood.'

Jumping to his feet he tripped
Into the tubs and all.
The food and drink and everything
Went flying in a sprawl.

And Nicholas and Alison
Though very occupied,
Could not ignore the noise they heard
Now coming from outside.

So throwing on some clothes they ran
Out into the street,
Doing all they could to hide
Their scheming and deceit.

'What's going on?' the people cried.
And then the crowd there saw
The sad, old carpenter flat out
Upon the barn's stone floor.

Before he had a chance to speak
And tell his sorry tale,
Both Nicholas and Alison
Began there to regale,

Their neighbours with a load of lies
About the carpenter.
They said just anything they could
To artfully infer,

The poor, old boy was off his head.
A half-wit and a dud
Who'd filled his mind with crazy thoughts
About another flood.

As bad as Noah's, maybe worse,
And then he'd made them both
Sit up all night within the barn –
They swore this under oath.

No matter what old John avowed,
However much he tried
To tell his story, everyone
Just said the poor fool lied.

And from that day it was believed,
(Though it was very sad),
That poor old John, the carpenter
Was off his head – quite mad.

Thus the canny Nicholas
Achieved his wicked way,
And Absolon, quite by mistake
The very self-same day,

Kissed his beloved Alison,
But sad to say, I fear
Not on her luscious ruby lips
But on her comely rear.

And on that day was Nicholas
Hot branded on his bum,
Which not surprising made the lad
Morose and very glum.

So now this tale is over,
It's well and truly done,
And so I say, 'God bless you all,
Long life to everyone!'

His shifty eye and angry glance
Were hidden by his hat

THE REEVE'S PROLOGUE

Now when the Miller's tale was done
Everyone agreed,
It was the funniest story that
They'd listened to indeed.

In truth, the most ridiculous
That they had ever heard.
The whole thing quite preposterous,
So foolish and absurd.

So when the Miller ceased to speak,
And for a long time after,
The motley band were all creased up
With riotous, loud laughter.

No-one seemed upset – except
Perhaps the ancient Reeve,
For he had been a carpenter –
He looked down at his sleeve,

His shifty eye and angry glance
Were hidden by his hat,
Then up he looked and said, 'Miller,
I'll pay you back for that.

'But I am old and can't abide
To quarrel anymore,
And yet I've got so much to tell,
Such stories in my store.'

And then he gave a sermon
Of life and its strange ways.
And how his course was nearly run –
About his former days.

He said, 'I'm just an old man now,
Most of my life is done,
And all my tales are of the past,
That's when I had my fun.'

Our Host on hearing Oswald speak,
(This was the old Reeve's name.)
Said, 'Come my friend and tell your tale
And join us in our game.'

So Oswald answered loud and clear,
'This Miller spoke with glee,
Poking fun at carpenters,
I was one once, you see.

'So I intend to pay him back
For his tale, so absurd,
For all his silly foolery,
For every filthy word.

'He knew what he was doing,
He was aware that he
When making fun of carpenters
Was making fun of me.

'He doesn't see the plank within
His eyes – yet sees the speck
In mine and for this selfishness
I'd gladly break his neck.'

And so the Reeve, old Oswald,
The Miller did regale,
Then smiling to himself he thus
Began to tell this tale.

And so these merry couples
Carried on this way

THE REEVE'S TALE

At Trumpington, down Cambridge way,
Beside a little hill,
Close by a gently running stream
There stood an ancient mill.

And in this mill some time ago
There lived a Miller who
Was really rather up himself –
He was a bully too.

And also proud as any man,
Bad-tempered too, I fear.
For those who weren't respectful – well,
He'd thump them on the ear.

He wore a vicious hunting knife
He wasn't scared to use,
So from this man it's fair to say
Malevolence did ooze.

For it was pretty widely known
This Miller often took
Corn and meal that wasn't his.
In short – he was a crook.

The Miller's wife was haughty for
Her father was a priest.
She'd never thought her life would be
Involved with grain and yeast.

Not for a moment had she thought
She'd wed a man of corn,
She was convinced she was well-bred
And very nobly born.

And so this pair would walk about
With noses in the air,
Despite the fact they were a crass
And quite dishonest pair.

They had a daughter, fine of face
And always nicely dressed.
Ample in her beam she was
And fulsome in her breast.

With golden hair and silky skin
And bright, red sexy lips,
She was a sight when she walked past
With her sashaying hips.

One other word must now be said –
She was a giving sort,
And given half a chance she would
Be game for any sport.

They also had a little boy,
A sunny, handsome lad,
Still a baby, just the sort
To make a cold heart glad.

So this then was the family
Of the Miller there,
And they all lived a happy life
Quite free of any care.

This Miller made his customers
Pay right through the nose.
For grinding wheat and grain and all,
He'd sneakily impose,

A price that was too high – in fact
He'd fiddle far too much,
And baffle people with his sums
That looked like double-Dutch.

There was a Cambridge college which
Is sadly long forgotten
Where this Miller plied his trade
And fiddled something rotten.

And then one day the Manciple
At the college there
Took sick and he was diagnosed
With something very rare.

The poor man went to bed and this
Was welcome, that's for sure
By the Miller who then stole
More than he had before.

In the past he'd been restrained
But now was of a mind
To con the college ruthlessly,
He robbed that college blind.

But then two lively students there
Thought one sunny morn
That they would watch the Miller as
He ground the college corn.

They thought it would be fun and said,
'We'll watch the sneaky devil,
And make quite sure that everything
Is straight and on the level.'

One of the students was called John,
Alan was the other.
They both came from a pleasant place
Known by the name of Strother.

And so they loaded all the corn
Onto a horse and cart.
Once this was done, they were prepared
To make an early start.

Arriving at the mill, they spoke,
'Good Miller, are you there?'
The Miller, Simon Simpkin came
And he addressed the pair.

'Hello young John and Alan too.'
His pleasantness ran rife.
They replied, 'And how are you,
And your good lady wife?'

And then they said, 'Our Manciple
Is very nearly dead.
Our corn needs grinding so he's sent
The pair of us instead.'

Now Simpkin thought, 'It makes no odds,
Both Alan and young John
Are gullible and will I'm sure
Be easy guys to con.'

But then the lads declared they wished
To watch their fine corn grind,
And Simpkin then pretended that
He really didn't mind.

But then John said, 'To make quite sure
That nothing goes a cropper,
I'd like to watch as all our corn
Is poured into the hopper.'

Then Alan spoke again and said,
'I'd like to watch the meal
Come out the bottom to ensure
We get a proper deal.'

The Miller Simpkin scratched his head
And smiled a knowing smile,
For after all he was renowned
For craftiness and guile.

He thought, 'These two are quite convinced
They'll get the best of me,
But they don't stand a chance, for that's
A thing you'll never see.

'I'll find a way to fix this pair
As only Simpkin can.
I'll find a way to substitute
Some of their flour for bran.

'For though they may be scholars
It doesn't count for much,
For sometimes there are working folk
Who have a wiser touch.'

And so without another word
He left the lads to guard
The hopper and the trough below –
And sidled to the yard.

Once there sly Simpkin looked around,
He saw he was alone
So walked up to the student's horse,
An ancient dappled roan.

And then with stealth he freed the horse
And then he let him go,
And that old horse just galloped off
As horses will, you know.

And then the Miller wandered back.
He never said a word.
Only later did the lads
Find out what had occurred.

When all the corn was ground and packed
In sacks and all was done,
They thought they'd get a breath of air
And watch the setting sun.

On walking out they gazed around
At trees and flowers and gorse,
And then they thought, 'Now something's wrong.
Oh crikey, where's the horse?'

'Our horse is gone,' they cried aloud.
The Miller with his wife
Came rushing from the mill and said,
'You're right, upon my life!'

'He's run off with the wild, free mares,'
The Miller's wife exclaimed.
'Those mares are quite unruly and
They never can be tamed.'

John and Alan standing there
Took very little heed.
Their thoughts were of their horse and so
They took off at great speed.

Determined now to find the horse,
That runaway, that hack,
And corner him and catch him – then
Bring the old fellow back.

So once they'd gone the Miller said,
'We'll take some of their stack
Of flour – for you to cook dear wife
Before the pair come back.

'They thought that they could lead me on
A merry, silly dance.
They thought that they could beat me but
They didn't stand a chance.'

And so he stole a bushel from
The sacks of college flour,
And gave it to his wife to use
Upon that very hour.

It was a whole lot later when
The two young lads returned.
They had the horse but in their hearts
An indignation burned.

They guessed that they had been set up
And also thought for sure
The Miller would have nicked their flour
And placed it in his store.

On arriving at the mill
They went then to enquire,
If they could stay the night – they found
The Miller by his fire.

They said, 'It's much too late to go
Back to Cambridge town,
So can we have a room to sleep?'
The Miller wore a frown.

'My mill is very small,' he said.
'I've only got one room,
But you are scholars and therefore
I guess I can presume

'That you are also gentlemen
So take a bed in there.
With me, my wife and daughter and
My baby, you may share.'

So once this all had been agreed,
They settled down to eat,
The Miller's wife had cooked a goose,
A really handsome treat.

And as they ate, they quaffed their ale,
And this of course then led
To each of them becoming drunk
And fuzzy in the head.

Come midnight they all made their way
Up to the room to bed.
'You lads can nod off over there,'
The sleepy Miller said.

So there they were, all in one room,
I swear upon my life.
The daughter in her bed alone,
The Miller with his wife.

And by their bed a cradle stood,
Their boy asleep inside,
And John and Alan shared a bed
Which wasn't very wide.

And so they settled down to sleep,
And then the Miller's jaw
Dropped down and with his wife as well
They both began to snore.

They'd taken so much booze on board
That when they snored, the sound
Did hit the walls and fill the room
And round the lads rebound.

Alan lying there beside
Young John, then pulled his jacket.
'In all your life, have you e'er heard
Such an awful racket?

'Anyway my mind is set
Upon one certain thing,
With the Miller's daughter there
I'm going to have a fling.

'I'll have my wicked way with her,
On this I've set my mind,
Ever since I saw her face
And her sweet, plump behind.

'This Miller here has nicked our flour
And there's a law you'll find,
That says if someone steals from you,
Then take it back in kind.

'So that is what I now will do.
I swear I'll have the daughter.'
John replied, 'Take care, for this
Could end up with your slaughter.

'The Miller is a fearsome man
And he will surely slay
Any man who tries to have
His selfish, wicked way,

'With the daughter whom he loves.
Take special care my friend,
Or this adventure could well prove
To be your sticky end.'

Well, Alan would not be deterred
And silently he crept
Across the room up to the bed
Wherein the young girl slept.

She lay there on the bed and then
That sneaky Alan there
Eased himself on top of her –
How could he even dare!

She woke with just a little start,
And thought, 'Oh this is fun.'
And so to put it tastefully,
In no time they were one.

Meanwhile John lay there in bed,
Of course, now on his own,
And all he heard as he lay there
Was the sweet daughter groan.

He thought, 'This is a fine to do.
Alan had no qualms,
And for his pain the rotter's got
The daughter in his arms.

'I'm the sucker here,' he thought,
'Just left out in the cold,
And I'll be laughed at that's for sure
If this night's work is told.'

So in the dark he rises then
And in the inky gloom,
He grasps the cradle by the bed
At t'other side of room.

He moves it then to sit beside
His own sad, lonesome bed.
'Now maybe something good will come,'
He resolutely said.

Once he was back, snug in his bed
The wife then ceased to snore,
And then she rose and left the room
By its great, oaken door.

When she returned she groped around,
Feeling for the cot,
When it wasn't there she thought,
'This cannot be the spot.

'Oh dearie me – I nearly jumped
Into another bed.'
And in the dark her features turned
The brightest shade of red.

She groped some more and then she found
The cradle, then she thought,
'This is our bed, it is the one
That in the dark I sought.'

So in she climbed and lay beside
Young John who was there waiting,
And thus she'd fallen blamelessly
For his quite naughty baiting.

John waited then for just a tick
Before he moved right in,
And once more in these tales we see
A case of carnal sin.

The Miller's wife had no idea
She'd chosen the wrong one,
And if she'd known, would she have cared?
For she was having fun.

And so these merry couples
Carried on this way,
Until they heard the cock cry out
Heralding the day.

Alan who'd been hard at work
Throughout the long, sweet night,
Said, 'Farewell Molly – you've been great,
But now I must take flight.'

'Goodbye my dear,' sweet Molly sighed,
'But heed before you go,
For there is something I must tell,
There's something you should know.

'Father stole your flour and then
Mother baked a cake.
So when you leave, I would suggest
That what is yours, you take.

'You'll find it by the mill's main door.
It's made with your own meal,
And I admit 'twas in a sack
That I helped father steal.'

Alan thanked her and then made
His way back to his bed,
But on his way he bumped into
The cradle and he said,

'I nearly made a bad mistake
For sleeping soundly there
Are the Miller and his wife,
I really must take care.'

And so he groped around the room –
It wasn't quite yet day,
And then he came upon the bed
In which the Miller lay.

He gently eased himself into
The bed beside the Miller,
And thinking it was John he said,
'This night has been a thriller.

'Three times in this short night I've had
The Miller's daughter fair,
And all the time the silly fool's
Been lying over there.'

'Well is that so?' the Miller cried.
'You dirty rotten swine.
You dare to come here and defile
My daughter, sweet and fine.'

He grabbed poor Alan by the throat
And they began to fight.
They heaved and punched and scratched and tore
With all their strength and might.

The Miller's face was drenched with blood
But still he fought some more,
Then in the midst of fighting,
He lurched across the floor.

He staggered backwards right onto
His satiated wife.
She was sleeping next to John
Unmindful of this strife.

He fell upon her heavily.
She woke up with a start.
She cried in panic desperately
And with a pounding heart.

She yelled for Simpkin, her dear spouse.
'Help, help, oh help me please.
Oh Simpkin save your loving wife,
I'm begging on my knees.

'The whole world has gone crazy here,
Each and every bit.'
She yelled and screamed and carried on
Like she was in a fit.

She jumped out from the bed and then
She grabbed from by the wall,
A stick she knew they kept right there –
Then stepped into the brawl.

Now it was still quite dark in there.
The dawn had not yet come.
But with the stick held high she stepped
Right back into the scrum.

A little chink of light crept in
And by it she then saw
Something white – she thought that is
A student's cap for sure.

She brought the great stick crashing down
With all her force and hate,
But it was not a student, 'twas
Her husband's shiny pate.

He cried out loud in agony
And then the two lads beat
The poor, old Miller half to death
And then made their retreat.

They grabbed their sacks of flour and took
The horse and laden cart,
Then grabbed the cake from by the door
And then made to depart.

They heard the Miller crying out
As they took off that day,
But they just laughed and coldly said,
There was a price to pay,

For being crooked and a thief –
He'd really got his due.
His wife and daughter had been had
And he'd been beaten too.

For as the ancient proverb says,
Evil comes to he
Who evil does and it's a fact
That's just how things will be.

'And so I say,' the Reeve proclaimed,
'Before you I have laid
My tale and yes, I think by gad
The Miller I've repaid.'

And so he laughed and roared with glee

THE COOK'S PROLOGUE

The Cook there in our happy throng
Laughed loudest of us all.
He said, 'By God, that Miller there
Took an almighty fall.

'He really got a seeing to,'
He merrily observed.
'By Christ's passion he did get
All things that he deserved.

'And surely there's a lesson here –
Take care to watch your spouse.
And never let a stranger stay
A night within your house.

'But if you do, well make quite sure
Of one thing most of all,
You get a house that's large enough
And not a house that's small.'

And so he laughed and roared with glee
And finally did say,
'I've never heard of anyone
Who got stitched up this way.

'We really cannot leave it here,
For someone else must don
The mantle of the raconteur
And so then carry on.

'And though I am impoverished,
A poor man – aye it's true,
I'm quite prepared to tell a tale
Which may amuse you too.

'It is about a merry jape
That happened in my town.'
Our Host cried, 'Let us hear it Cook
Before the sun goes down.

'Come on Roger, tell us all
For we can hardly wait.'
And thus this is the tale the Cook
Began then to relate.

Any time of day or night
This lad was up for fun

THE COOK'S TALE

There was a young apprentice in
The food trade in our town,
His hair was black, a merry soul,
With face of berry brown.

He was so fond of having fun
And partying and all,
That he was called 'the reveller' –
For him life was a ball.

And any chance he had to play
He'd just down tools and run.
Any time of day or night
This lad was up for fun.

He loved the ladies, that's a fact.
He loved them very well,
But he was lustful in his way
If truth we are to tell.

He liked to sing and dance and drink –
He thought this very nice,
And sadly he was far too keen
On gambling with dice.

His flippant manner caused him strife.
His boss found him a pain,
And told him off relentlessly
Time and time again.

At last his boss had had enough
And argued to himself,
'A rotten apple soon infects
The others on the shelf.

'So best to throw the apple out
Where it cannot attack
All the others,' – so he gave
The lazy lad the sack.

The former 'prentice now was free
To play all night and day,
And so he went to see a friend
Who played the self-same way.

And then he said unto this friend
With his most winning smile,
'I've lost my job, I need a bed.
May I stay here a while?'

His friend agreed, so he moved in –
This friend – he had a wife,
And I must here relate that she
Let naughtiness run rife,

For though she ran a little shop
They were quite destitute,
And so to top their coffers up
She was a prostitute...

But at this point a cry went up,
High-pitched and very shrill,
And everybody's thought was that
Somebody must be ill.

But it was just the Parson who
Spoke sternly to the Cook.
'All this filth and wantonness
Is something I'll not brook.'

He puffed and blew and spluttered too,
He looked extremely vexed.
'The trouble with the lot of you
Is that you're oversexed...

'Lewd things are all you think about,'
He said with angry stare.
'By rights your thoughts should be consumed
With piety and prayer.

'When our good Host suggested that
We each might tell a tale
I thought that all the people here
Would surely then regale

'The company with tales about
Our Saviour, Christ the Lord,
I surely thought that everyone
Would be of this accord.

'I thought that each of us would be
Joined – as by a bridge,
For after all, each one of us
Is on a pilgrimage.

'We travel now to Canterbury,
Unto that holy shrine,
And surely as we make our way
Our thoughts should all entwine,

'And then be concentrated on
The goodness of the Lord,
For then his grace and sanctity
Will be our just reward.'

The Cook went very red indeed.
Was this embarrassment?
Or was he really angry at
The Parson's harassment.

And then he yelled, ''Twas but some fun,
And no more tasteless than
The Miller's tale, so why should you
Try to impose a ban?'

The company all then began
To shout and talk at once.
Some said the Cook was just a fool,
A silly chap – a dunce.

And others said the Parson there
Was just a silly prude,
And said the Cook's tale sounded good
And really not too rude.

The noise of shouting got so loud
That our good Host cried out.
He really had to yell with force –
My word he had to shout.

But finally they quietened down –
Our Host in his grand style
Turned to the Cook and softly said,
'Best leave it for a while.

'I know you have a jolly tale
That's full of carnal fun,
But my advice is back off now
Before some harm is done.

'Maybe later you can tell
Your lusty tale but now
I think it best to make quite sure
That we avoid a row.'

The Cook just muttered sullenly,
'My tale had such a twist.'
And others there looked quite annoyed
About the tale they'd missed.

But the Parson's smile was broad
And he looked mighty smug,
Clearly he was very pleased
That he had pulled the rug

Out from underneath the Cook.
He'd been quite right, he knew.
And so he crossed himself and said,
''Twas proper thing to do.'

*'I haven't got the wit to speak
In our friend Chaucer's way.'*

THE MAN OF LAW'S PROLOGUE

One day around the hour of ten
Our Host looked at the sky
And said, 'By yonder tilt of sun
It seems that time does fly.

'Once time has flown it ne'er returns –
I'm sure you've heard this told,
That once it's gone it's lost for good,
Unlike a pot of gold.

'For gold that's lost can then be found,
But I am much a-feared,
That time is gone forever once
It's past and disappeared.

'It's like young Molly's maidenhead,
Once gone, I have to say,
She cannot get it back – it's gone,
For wantonness – you pay.

'Anyway, enough of that
For we do waste our time,
And that is something which I feel
Is tantamount to crime.

'And so my honest Man of Law,
You said you'd tell a tale,
So speak my friend as we go on,
Up hill and down through dale.

'For you have been contracted to
Relate a tale to us.'
The Man of Law said, 'So I shall,
And gladly without fuss.

'For I agreed to join your game
And that is what I'll do.
Not for a moment would I think
Of trying to undo

'That to which I gave my word
But I must frankly say,
I haven't got the wit to speak
In our friend Chaucer's way.

'For in his time he's told such tales,
And so many too,
He's hardly left a tale untold
For each of us to do.

'Such stories of adventure,
Of love and lust and crimes,
All told in measured metre and
All using clever rhymes.

'Thus friend Chaucer, I'll not try
To imitate, for he
Will always beat me at this game
And get the best of me.

'So now I'll tell this tale of mine,
In my straightforward way.'
Then he began and this is what
The good man had to say.

And so the ship then sailed away

THE MAN OF LAW'S TALE

My tale is set in days of old
And tells of merchant men
Who'd buy and sell and barter and
Sort out deals and then

Export all kinds of items
To lands across the seas,
Their purpose was to gain great wealth
To fund a life of ease.

But then one day some merchants said,
'It may be fine at home,
But even so let's have a go
At plying trade in Rome.'

So off they went and once ensconced
Within that famous town,
They said, 'Let's get to know this place.'
So ventured up and down

Throughout the city streets and lanes,
Down avenues, through squares.
Each went about his business and
They sorted their affairs.

They hadn't been in town that long
When they all heard about
The Emperor's daughter Constance who
'Twas said – without a doubt,

Was full of goodness and that she
Was hailed both far and wide
For being kind and virtuous
And quite devoid of pride.

Truly lovely, she would make
Somebody such a bride.
The girl was flawless, she must be
A saint personified.

Before they left to go back home
The merchants went to see
This lovely girl and all agreed
That she must surely be,

The fairest maid in all the world,
None other could compare
With lovely Constance, whom they saw
Serenely sitting there.

But now their ships were filled with goods,
They hurriedly set sail,
And on arriving home they rushed
To then recount the tale,

Of all their great adventures,
Of everything they'd done
To their country's Sultan who
Ruled over everyone.

He loved to hear of foreign lands –
And so the merchants went
To tell him of the wonders and
About the time they'd spent

Exploring Rome – and everything
That they had seen and heard.
The Sultan listened eagerly
To each and every word.

And then they told him all about
The lovely girl they'd seen,
The daughter of the Emperor,
And he did all to glean

Every detail of this girl –
And so they told him how
She shone with goodness and with charm
And then to him did vow,

That she would make the loveliest
Bride in all the world,
And as they spoke of Constance there,
The Sultan's love unfurled,

Until he vowed with certainty,
'I swear by God above
Although I've never seen this girl
She is the one I'll love.'

And so he called his counsellors,
The wise men of his court,
And told them all in feverish tones
The end that he now sought.

He said, 'I want this Constance
To be here by my side,
For I will never ever rest
Until she is my bride.

'And if I cannot have her
To be my dearest wife,
I fear I'll perish so give thought
On how to save my life.'

His mentors there all racked their brains,
And said, 'The only way
Was to give Rome's Emperor
Much gold and also say,

'The Sultan would live by the rules
Of Romans, then perhaps
Any doubts that he might have
Would crumble and collapse.'

And so negotiations then
Took place and in short time,
It was agreed – the Sultan said,
'This all is quite sublime.'

But in Rome 'twas not the same,
Poor Constance there did weep,
And all night long she tossed and turned
And couldn't get to sleep.

And she addressed the Emperor,
She said, 'Oh, father dear,
To leave our fair, beloved Rome
Is something that I fear.

'And once I've gone, I'll never see
Rome or you again.'
But Emperors can be severe
And he ignored her pain.

He said, 'You should be grateful girl!'
For this was way back when
Daughters did what father said
As girls were ruled by men.

And so the day arrived when she,
Poor Constance said goodbye,
But she was stoic and resolved
For royal folk don't cry.

Her family were gathered there,
And all they said was this.
'Goodbye Constance.' That was all.
They gave no parting kiss.

And then her ship unfurled its sails,
It left the Roman shore,
Brave Constance stood there regally
And quietly she bore,

The sadness beating in her heart
For her receding home,
Quite certain now that ne'er again
Would she see mighty Rome.

Now the Sultan had a mother
Who wasn't very nice,
And she expected her dear son
To take her sound advice,

About most things – but most of all
On matters of the heart,
So when she heard what he now planned
She sat up with a start.

'This cannot be,' she cried with rage.
Oh how her mind did foam.
She was in tumult and declared,
'We want no truck with Rome.'

The Sultan wouldn't heed her words.
He said, 'It's not for you
To say who should become my wife,
That is for me to do.'

And so she called some men of rank.
'Now listen well,' she said.
'My son thinks he's in love and plans
A Roman girl to wed.

'This shall not stand. It cannot pass.
This really shall not be.
We do not want to take their ways,
'Twould be the death of me.

'But for the moment we'll pretend
To go along with this.
I'll tell my son that I agree
And seal it with a kiss.'

And so she went to see her son,
And said to him, 'My dear,
I'm happy for you now to wed.'
And then she made it clear,

That she would take the Roman path
And not stand in his way.
The Sultan hugged his mother then
And cried, 'You've made my day.'

She kissed her son and hugged him too
And so with happy heart,
He shouted out exuberantly,
'Let celebrations start.'

Meanwhile fair Constance sailed the seas,
To her new home she came.
The Sultan met his bride to be,
His passions all a-flame.

He'd told his people, 'Come with me.'
And asked his mother too.
You can I'm sure imagine that
It was all quite a do.

With banners flying in the air
Of every cast and hue,
And then the moment waited for –
The bride came into view.

She was stunning, beautiful,
With such a regal air –
Up stepped the Sultan's mother then –
Sweet Constance should beware!

But no, the mother treated her
As if she loved her well,
She held her closely – no-one there
In any way could tell,

That she was making evil plans
As she stood warmly there,
Poor Constance didn't have a clue
That she should take great care.

Then the Sultan came before
The girl who'd be his wife,
He bowed to her and vowed that he
Would love her all his life.

And then most happily he took
Fair Constance to his home.
He said, 'You'll be as happy here,
As e'er you were in Rome.'

At long last the time approached
For the wedding day,
Everything was in its place,
Such gold there on display.

And dishes quite as sumptuous
As any ever seen,
A setting quite befitting
A sultan, king or queen.

Everything had been arranged
By the Sultan's mother,
But 'twould have been the best by far
If planned by someone other.

This evil woman, this old crone.
This harridan, this shrew.
This vixen, ogress, harpy, witch,
Was now about to do,

A really quite horrendous thing,
The thought just turns you pale.
It makes you shake and tremble and
Recoil and flinch and quail.

For once the guests were sitting down
And ready to take food,
They little thought that this would be
But just a brief prelude,

To quite the most cold-blooded
Carnage ever seen,
And all of it ordained and planned
By that foul hag, so mean.

For just as they were starting
To eat a dish of cod,
The ogress surreptitiously
Gave a sneaky nod.

This then was the signal
For her horrific sin,
It was a sign for butchery
And mayhem to begin.

For then a band of lethal men
Fell on the party there,
And very few who ate that day
Did these foul butchers spare.

And everyone who had agreed –
Each woman and each man,
Who'd said they'd take the Roman way
To aid the Sultan's plan,

Was hacked to death or stabbed right through
Right there just where they ate,
Some with bloodied heads just fell
Face down upon their plate.

And Romans lost their lives as well,
They too were slaughtered there,
The Sultan also lost his life,
His mother didn't care,

For now she planned to rule herself.
She'd take the Sultan's place,
So as she watched the slaughtering
A wry smile crossed her face.

But what of Constance you may ask?
Was she killed in the fray?
What was planned to be her fate
Upon that frightful day?

Well it may be the mother was
Afraid of mighty Rome,
Because she spared the girl and said,
'I'm sending you back home.'

She placed poor Constance on a ship,
A manky vessel too,
And said, 'Get out of here, my girl
Before I change my view.'

She put some treasure on the ship
Along with ample food,
And Constance went aboard, quite numb,
And totally subdued.

She prayed unto the Lord above
And begged, 'Please keep me strong.'
She said, 'Stay with me now dear Lord
As you have all along.'

And so the ship then sailed away
And I must tell I fear,
It bounced around upon the seas
For several months that year.

And all this time sweet Constance
Kept her faith and trust,
In just the way that she'd been told
That all good Christians must.

And like good Constance, that old ship
Was true and didn't falter,
Until one day it journeyed through
The Straits of proud Gibraltar.

Then fearsome winds caught that small ship
And strongly pushed it forth
Into the raging ocean where
They drove it to the north.

Onwards the ship was driven
As if by unseen hand,
Till it was washed up on the coast
Of cold Northumberland.

There was a castle just close by,
The man in charge was called
The Constable – he was concerned
And really quite appalled

To see a ship washed up on shore.
He thought, 'I'd better check
To see if anyone's survived
That quite horrendous wreck.'

And when he found young Constance – well
His heart went out to her.
He brought her safely to the shore.
She said, 'I thank you sir.'

He took her to the castle,
And grateful for her life,
She became good friends with him
And Hermengild, his wife.

As time passed by they grew so close
And Hermengild would say,
That she loved Constance very much
And hoped that she would stay.

Thus the time passed happily
Until a dreadful day
When the castle's Constable
Had to go away.

He had to go and see the King.
King Alla was his name.
And while away a lustful knight
Was set upon a game.

This knight had tried his very best
To woo sweet Constance there,
But she had no desire at all
To start on an affair.

However much he tried his luck,
He found on each occasion
That she would just reject his pleas,
Resisting all persuasion.

For she was sweet and pure and true
And he was base and low,
So however much he tried
She didn't want to know.

Then when the knight became aware
The Constable was gone,
Within his mind, it must be said
A selfish light went on.

He thought, 'This is my chance to get
Revenge and pay her back.'
And as he spoke his face turned dark,
Like thunder it was black.

She'd spurned him so he'd be avenged.
He acted out of spite.
And then he thought, 'I'll do it now.
I'll sort her out tonight.

'If Constance will not be my love,
Give me what I desire,
Well then she'll pay.' His very soul
Was burning like a fire.

So he crept to the castle keep
At dark and dead of night.
He felt his way for at that time
There was but little light.

Sweet Constance was in bed, asleep,
Worn out from constant prayer,
And close to her good Hermengild
Was softly sleeping there.

The fiend crept to the bedroom, then
With gleaming knife he smote
The sleeping Hermengild and then
He slit the lady's throat.

And then he laid the blood-soaked knife
By sleeping Constance there,
To thus imply her guilt – dear God
How life can be unfair.

Next day the Constable returned
And with him came the King,
And oh what dreadful wailing when
They saw this awful thing.

For there was Hermengild, quite dead,
That much adored, sweet wife,
And Constance now stood there accused
Of taking her poor life.

They dragged scared Constance to the King,
She stood there in his sight.
Accused of this foul act, by who?
Why by that dreadful knight.

He said, 'She killed dear Hermengild
And so should pay the price.'
Without a doubt he was a fiend
Wrapped in a web of vice.

Poor Constance wept and prayed and fell,
Down onto her knees,
And surely the most stony heart
Would listen to her pleas.

She said, 'Oh dearest God on high,
I've given no offence,
I know you know of my pure heart
And of my innocence.

'Yet here I stand with nobody
To speak or plead for me,
It seems to suffer grievous wrong
Is now my destiny.

'I have no friends to show me care
Or indeed to fashion
My defence – or show an ounce
Of kindness or compassion.'

King Alla looked upon the girl
And tears came to his eyes,
He knew for sure that someone there
Was truly telling lies.

But was it Constance, that sweet lass,
Or was it someone other?
Had the awful deed been done
By her or by another?

He was a decent king and looked
At this poor girl so pretty,
And as he had a kindly heart
He felt a deal of pity.

He saw her staring hopelessly
There within his sight,
And by her side he saw her foe,
That black and evil knight.

And so it was King Alla then
Sternly told them both,
'There's just one way to settle this –
The knight must swear an oath.

'And if he swears that Constance here
Put Hermengild to death,
Well then this wretched maiden
Will draw her final breath.

'For she will face the axe-man's blade
And he'll strike off her head,
For if she is a murderess,
Well then, she should be dead.'

They brought a huge, great leather book,
The Gospels writ inside,
And everybody strained to see
Just who it was who'd lied.

The knight then placed his hand upon
The book and swore that she –
Young Constance was the guilty one
And never should be free.

He cried, 'She killed poor Hermengild,
She was the one who spilt
Her precious blood.' And thus the knight
Did testify her guilt.

Now spirits sometimes intervene,
And was this now the case?
For something happened that brought fear
To everybody's face.

For as he spoke a hand appeared,
It came from just thin air.
It struck the knight a sprawling blow
That sent him flying there.

And then a booming voice spoke out,
'You have defamed this child.
A daughter of the church – foul rogue,
Her name you have defiled.

'For she is innocent and pure,
'Twas you who did this deed,
And so King Alla, all of you
I tell you now, take heed,

'And turn to Christ with reverence.
I tell you, bow your face,
And then forever more you will
Reside in his sweet grace.'

Well that was really quite enough
To seal the foul knight's fate,
He very quickly paid the price
For all his lustful hate.

They took him out and he was slain
And then the King did say,
The knight deserved to die and in
This quick, no-nonsense way.

He looked at Constance then and thought,
'It's time that I came clean.'
So said, 'I love you Constance dear,
I want you for my queen.'

In shock, she now accepted this
Unforeseen proposal,
And told King Alla, that of course
She was at his disposal.

And in truth she liked him well
But there was one who fumed,
King Alla's mother, Donegild
With anger was consumed.

She didn't want her handsome son,
Her little boy – her pearl,
To marry someone foreign, he
Should wed a British girl.

Poor Constance she had such bad luck,
(And we don't know the cause.)
She wasn't very good at all
At choosing mother-in-laws.

But still the wedding went ahead
Despite this new-found foe,
And it was really marvellous,
A quite tremendous show.

And then a short time after this,
Fair Constance, sweet and mild,
Had some very happy news
For she was now with child.

And as the time approached when this
Sweet baby would be born,
The King set off for Scotland on
One cold and frosty morn.

He had affairs of state to fix –
He'd not be gone that long.
So Constance lay and waited for
Her child to come along.

And then one day the child arrived.
Oh what a scene of joy,
For Constance was the mother of
A bonny, baby boy.

She called him Maurice and 'twas said
A message must now go
To Scotland, there to tell the King,
They had to let him know.

And so a messenger was tasked
To go there with all speed,
To Scotland and to tell the King –
But now take special heed,

For this messenger ignored
All that he had been told,
And took himself to Donegild
And there he did unfold

The details of the birth and how
King Alla had a son,
And Donegild thought to herself,
'This needs to be undone.'

'I cannot let this stand,' she breathed.
And then she turned and said,
'Take food and wine good messenger
Then get yourself to bed,

'For you can travel on the morn
But rest yourself tonight.'
And thus it was when he'd retired
And was well out of sight,

That Donegild, that awful wretch
Wrote another note,
A very clever forgery,
And this is what she wrote.

'Dear King Alla, we must tell
Of the most awful thing
That ever has occurred to serf,
Or merchant man or king.

'How can we give the news to you?
But sadly we must tell,
The Queen, your wife, has given birth
To something out of hell.

'A creature really horrible.
A fiend! A ghoul! – Oh King!
A creature out of fiery hell,
A truly dreadful thing.

'This Constance must be damned for sure –
A monstrous creature who
Comes from the underworld – and she
Is evil through and through.'

Thus the altered note was sent
To poor King Alla who
On seeing it cried out in pain,
'This surely can't be true!'

He prayed to God, his face creased by
Disbelief and anguish.
And then he said, 'Yon messenger,
Take heed, this is my wish.

'Take this note writ in my hand
Back to my wife and court,
And say that though this grievous news
Had made me most distraught,

'I hereby order that all care
Be shown unto my son
And to my wife.' – And then he said,
'Please see that this is done.'

He gave the messenger his note
And said, 'Now tell them pray
That I'll be home in but short weeks,
And so be on your way.'

But no surprise, that messenger
On leaving him that day,
Headed straight to Donegild –
That's where he made his way.

And once again she filled him up
With wine and then she stole
The note and changed it carefully –
Skulduggery her goal.

She wrote, 'King Alla here decrees
His wife must leave this land,
And never more return and this
Is signed by royal hand.

'Her son and she must both be placed
Upon the very ship
On which she came to these, our shores,
And let there be no slip,

'For she must leave within three days
And never more return.'
As Donegild there scribed this note
With hate, her soul did burn.

For she wrote to the Constable,
'If not done, you'll be flung
Into a loathsome dungeon and
Then very quickly hung.'

The messenger was then sent forth
With this new false decree
To tell the Constable to cast
Poor Constance on the sea.

And when the Constable there read
This awful, dreadful note,
He wrung his hands, he beat his chest,
His furrowed brow he smote.

'How can this be?' he cried aloud.
'Oh Lord God tell me why?
For if I disobey the King
He says that I will die.'

Oh how the people wailed as well,
For Constance, so petite,
Was cherished there by everyone
Because she was so sweet.

But there was nothing could be done
But cast her off once more.
The order from the King had said
She must leave Britain's shore.

So once again poor Constance there
Was taken to her ship.
She walked on board, her head held high,
Her child safe in her grip.

And as the ship sailed out to sea
She gazed back with a sigh,
A tear fell on her cheek, she breathed,
'Cruel husband, so goodbye.'

The ship was stocked with food – enough
To get her safely home,
For there was but one place to go –
She would return to Rome.

Meanwhile King Alla made his way
Back homewards once again,
Determined now to stay at home
And nobly there to reign.

On arriving back he asked
To see his wife and son,
The Constable with fearful heart
Told all that had been done.

He said, 'My Lord, I swear in faith
I always have been true,
And so I just deferred to all
You told me I must do.

'Your letter said, on pain of death
I must without delay,
Send your dear wife, sweet Constance and
Your little boy away.'

And then he showed the King the note,
The poor man shook with fear.
The King said, 'Bring the messenger.'
He ordered, 'Bring him here.'

The messenger was brought and he
In but a little time,
Told King Alla everything
Which showed his mother's crime.

And when the King again looked at
The note, he saw for sure,
It looked just like his mother's hand.
The King required no more.

His face now turned to thunder.
The whole court held their breath.
He said, 'Though she's my mother
I'll have her put to death.'

And from that awful edict
King Alla never swerved,
For she was executed
So got what she deserved.

King Alla now was so borne down
At loss of wife and child,
His anguish knew no bounds, his thoughts
Were bleak and ran most wild.

For there could never be relief
For this unhappy King
For all that had now come to pass,
For this appalling thing.

But what of Constance and her child?
How were the babe and she?
Fighting for their lives out there
Upon that raging sea.

Well she was trapped within a storm
And it did blow and roar
Till finally it drove the ship
Onto a foreign shore,

Close by a castle – folk came down
To check the vessel out.
But sad to say the steward there
Was something of a lout.

For when his lustful eyes fell on
Young Constance standing there,
He thought, 'I've seldom ever seen
A maiden quite so fair.'

He tried to have his wicked way
By using force, I fear,
But once again Christ intervened,
For he was ever near.

For in the struggle Constance pushed
The steward overboard,
And surely this was all contrived
By no-one but the Lord.

For when young Constance fought the man
It was a combat like
David and Goliath – for
With but a single strike,

She sent him flying from the ship
And then the scoundrel drowned,
His body sank beneath the waves
And it was never found.

Her ship sailed on until it reached
The Mediterranean sea,
And then by chance – or was it that
The good Lord made it be?

She met a vessel also bound
For home in Italy.
Whose captain said to Constance then,
'You must come back with me.

'You should not sail the seas alone
So let me take you home,
To my fair land of Italy,
To where I live in Rome.'

Poor Constance was most grateful
And went aboard his ship,
And she was treated kindly for
The last part of her trip.

The captain was a senator
And was just coming back
From a far-off country where
He'd made a bold attack.

For he'd avenged the wickedness
Of nobody other
Than the witch we met before,
The Sultan's evil mother.

He'd taught her such a lesson
For murdering her son
And all the Romans there as well –
And now the job was done,

He travelled home in triumph
Safe in the knowledge still
That mighty Rome had triumphed,
That he had done her will!

On their arrival safe in Rome
Fair Constance went to live
With the senator and his wife
And they did all to give,

Succour, comfort and a home
To Constance and her boy,
To try and bring a little hope,
And maybe even joy,

To this sad girl who'd borne so much
In such a stoic way.
They said, 'You're welcome in our home
So please feel free to stay.'

And so time passed and then great news,
A famous King had come
To Rome – and how the people cheered
And wildly beat the drum.

He'd come to pay his penance to
The Pope who sat in Rome.
He'd travelled many long, hard miles
From his far distant home.

For he had come from Britain and
It was no other than
King Alla – that most upright King,
That good and decent man.

A feast was thrown to welcome there
King Alla – Constance sent
Maurice, her son, to pay respects,
Before the King he bent.

When Alla saw the child he gasped,
The senator then said,
'The mother of this child is here,
I think his father's dead.'

'But tell me of his mother, please.'
King Alla asked with hope.
All thoughts of paying penance now
And bowing to the Pope

Had left his mind – he was intent
On finding out much more
About the mother of this boy.
He thought, 'I can't be sure,

'But this young boy is truly like
My Constance, could it be
That she is still alive and lives
Right here in Italy?'

The senator spoke up and said,
'His mother is so fine,
And pure and oh so virtuous,
And all this does combine,

'With sultry beauty of a kind
That you so seldom see.
If you would like to meet her Sire,
Well, come back home with me.'

188

Thus King Alla made his way
To meet the lovely girl,
And as he went, it's true to say
His heart was in a whirl.

When he arrived, the senator
Went speedily to bring
Fair Constance from her quarters
To meet the noble King.

When she was told King Alla stood
Waiting there to meet
The mother of sweet Maurice she
Grew wobbly on her feet.

With trepidation now she went
To see the husband who
Had sent her packing shamelessly,
She trembled through and through.

When Alla saw his lovely wife
His heart felt fit to break.
A tear rolled down his handsome face –
He spoke – his voice did quake.

'It was not I who used you so
And sent you thus away.
It was my mother exiled you
Upon that dreadful day.

'Let God above bear witness
I'm guiltless – not the one
Who exiled you,' – and then he told
What Donegild had done.

When Constance had absorbed the truth,
Oh then what boundless joy,
She hugged her husband – he in turn
Hugged her and their dear boy.

Once they were fully reconciled
She asked her husband to
Perform a favour, for she asked
If he would go and do

But one small thing – 'Oh please request
An invitation now
To dine there with the Emperor,
And ask if he'll allow,

'For extra guests – arrange to take
Your wife and handsome son.'
King Alla said he would and then
In no time it was done.

So came the day, when they were set
To go to Rome's great court,
To see the Emperor, Constance thus
Achieved the end she sought.

And when she stood before the man,
The Emperor of all
The Roman Empire – to her knees
Sweet Constance then did fall.

She said, 'Dear father, it is I,
Your own beloved daughter
Who went away and then survived
That awful, bloody slaughter.'

The Emperor looked upon his girl
Then bore her to her feet,
And joyfully the party went
Inside the court to eat.

So as this tale draws to a close,
There's not much more to say,
Except to add King Alla took
His wife and son away.

Back to Britain, there to live
A happy, quiet life,
Though Alla had but little time
To share with son and wife.

Scant chance to get to know his son
Or to be there beside
Sweet Constance – for within a year
Poor King Alla died.

Constance was distraught and sad.
With heaviness of heart
She once again got set to leave –
For Rome she would depart.

And so with Maurice by her side
She made her lonesome way,
Back to Rome, determined now
That that is where she'd stay.

And there she lived in piety,
Glad to be back home.
Until in time young Maurice was
Made Emperor of Rome.

And thus this brings now to an end
This sorry tale of old.
And then the Man of Law exclaimed,
'If I may be so bold,

'I do commend you to the Lord
To keep you in his grace,
And yes, I do mean everyone
Gathered in this place!'

'We don't want preaching and such things,
A sermon we don't need.'

EPILOGUE TO THE MAN OF LAW'S TALE

The Man of Law then ceased to speak,
His tale had run its course.
Our Host smiled widely and exclaimed
As he sat on his horse,

'Well, that was really something friend.
Oh what a tale you tell.
A matchless tale, a faultless tale.
Our game is going well.'

And then he turned towards the group
And there addressed the Priest.
'And now good sir it's time for you
To give us all a feast.

'For men of learning know such tales
To teach and to amuse,
And so dear priest commence at once,
There is no time to lose.'

Oh how our Host did flatter him.
He said, 'What tales you've got.
So start.' But then the Shipman cried,
'By heaven he shall not.

'We don't want preaching and such things,
A sermon we don't need.
So listen up for I've a tale
That everyone should heed.

'There won't be any holy stuff
Or philosophising,
And nothing on communion
Or about baptising.

'And nowt in Latin, that's for sure,
And nowt of Christ's great glory.
No mine is but a simple tale,
A quite straightforward story.'

So he sat in his counting house

THE SHIPMAN'S TALE

A merchant who was rich once lived
In St Denys and he
Was thought to be quite bright because
Of his great wealth you see.

Some people think that being rich
Denotes intelligence.
How else could people gain such wealth,
It can't be all pretence.

They must be clever, so it was
That everybody said,
The merchant of fair St Denys
Had sharp brains in his head.

So as my tale unfurls dear friends
You can then all decide
If this was true or had the folk
Been taken for a ride.

Now this rich merchant had a wife
For whom he cared a lot,
And she was lovely to behold,
On this I kid you not.

A fair complexion quite as fine
As any ever seen,
Long flaxen hair and eyes that shone
The colour of sea green.

And buxom too it must be said,
A comely lass for sure.
I think you get the general thrust
So I need say no more.

The merchant loved to entertain,
He filled his house with folk,
And in amongst his many guests
Was one good-looking bloke.

He was a Monk and he was then
As far as folk could gauge
A man around the region of
Some thirty years in age.

So friendly in his attitude,
So full of charm and grace,
And everyone was quite beguiled
By his warm, handsome face.

The merchant always welcomed him
With friendly open arms,
Like everybody else he was
Enraptured by his charms.

This handsome Monk whose name was John
Just loved to spend his cash,
He'd throw it round most lavishly,
He loved to make a splash.

So he was very popular
For when he came to call
He'd tip the servants and make sure
He gave to one and all.

But then one day the merchant said,
'I have to make a trip.
I've business I must see to – and
I'm off to Bruges township.'

And so he asked his friend, Monk John
If he would come on down
To keep an eye on his good wife
While he was out of town.

John was delighted and arrived
With not an hour's delay.
He said, 'I'll gladly watch your wife
The time you are away.'

Was there a hint of mischief as
The saintly Monk John spoke?
Perhaps he wasn't totally
A fair and decent bloke.

The merchant said, 'I'll leave for Bruges
Within a day or two.
Before I go, I would suggest
That this is what we do.

'You should relax and spend some time
With my good wife, for I
Must catch up with some paperwork.'
He said this with a sigh.

'I must ensure I'm not in debt
And balance my accounts.
And I must make quite sure that I
Have billed the right amounts.'

So off he went to count his cash –
He also undertook
To go through every entry in
His great big ledger book.

Each transaction that he'd made
Was written down in there,
And every one he scrutinised
With conscientious care.

So he sat in his counting-house
Well set to spend the day,
Surrounded by huge piles of cash
And invoices to pay.

He worked with care to ascertain
Was he in debt or not?
It was important that he knew
Just how much cash he'd got.

But then next day events moved on,
For in the garden there
The good Monk John was just about
To take the morning air.

And as he walked he came upon
The merchant's wife who said,
'Dear John, you are up early – why
Are you not still in bed?'

He replied, 'I've always found
Five hours sleep sufficient
To keep me fresh and quite alert,
Sharp-eyed and most efficient.

'But you my dear, you look tired out,
It seems that my good friend,
Your husband has been hard at work
All night – from start to end.

'You ought to go and rest awhile.'
What a salacious bloke!
And then he laughed out heartily
At this his tasteless joke.

The merchant's wife just shook her head,
'It's not like that at all.
The pleasure that I get from life
Is really very small.

'Across the whole of France there's not
A wife who bears my pain.
I rue the day that I was born
O'er and o'er again.

'If only I could leave this place.
Go far away,' she said.
'Or kill myself – I truly wish
Sometimes that I were dead.'

The Monk was most astounded and
His jaw dropped open wide,
'To see you in a state like this
I really can't abide.

'Confide in me and tell me all
For maybe I can find
A way to help you.' – 'John,' she said
'You're truly very kind.'

He urged, 'Now tell me everything,
And what you tell will be
A secret that I'll never breathe –
It will be safe with me.'

She sighed intensely, 'If I told
The details of my life,
You'd be amazed what I've endured
To be my husband's wife.

'But he's your friend – I should not speak,
You would not want to know.
To criticise a husband is
Considered base and low.'

The good Monk John then blurted out,
'He's not my friend, my dear.
For I love you, you are the draw,
The reason I come here.

'Tell me your troubles and your woes
While he works up above.'
She grasped his hands and kissed him and
She cried, 'Oh John – my love!

'I shouldn't really speak about
That worthless spouse of mine,
And if I did, then I should say
He's upright, good and fine.

'But truthfully he is a cur,
A mean and awful type.
Oh dear I feel so guilty when
I criticise and snipe.

'But why should I dissemble thus,
Distort the truth and lie
When I know plainly and for sure
That he's not worth a fly.

'All women want their spouse to be
Respectful,' she then said.
'Generous and kind of heart –
Considerate in bed.

'But most of all they need to know
They won't stint on the cash,
That they'll bale out a wife if she
Has overspent – been rash.

'And that dear John is what I've done,
And I will get no thanks
From my mean husband if he finds
I owe a hundred francs.

'He won't say, "Don't fret my dear,
I will attend to that."
No, he will call me stupid, crass,
A guttersnipe – a brat.

'Oh dear Monk John, you can assist,
Lend me the money please,
For those to whom the money's owed
Are putting on the squeeze.

'And if my husband hears of this
Or folk round here find out,
My reputation will be shot
And be reduced to nowt.

'But if you help me, well sweet John,'
She said seductively,
'I will be most appreciative,
And grateful, yes – you'll see.

'For if there is some little thing
I can do in return,
Well ask it.' – Now it doesn't take
A brain-box to discern,

Just what she meant, so John replied,
'Fret not for I'll help you.'
He grasped her by her buttocks then
And kissed her hotly too.

He said, 'Just leave all this to me.
I'll get the francs today.'
Then patting her across the rump
He sent her on her way.

Well, later on he up and spoke
Unto the merchant who
Was getting ready for his trip –
He said, 'My friend – will you

'Do this poor Monk a favour please
And very kindly lend
A hundred francs – and do it as
A favour for a friend?

'I need to buy some stores and though
'Twill be for just a week
I hope dear friend, you will not think
I've got enormous cheek.'

The merchant smiled and said, 'Dear John
The loan will be just fine,
I am delighted thus to help –
The pleasure is all mine.

'Just pay me back when e'er you can,
There isn't any hurry.
Do take your time and please my friend
I beg you not to worry.'

The Monk requested that the loan
Should be a secret for
He didn't want the folk round there
To think that he was poor.

The merchant readily agreed,
Then went to get the cash,
He wouldn't miss a hundred francs
From his impressive stash.

And so a day or two then passed –
The merchant, that poor stooge
Packed up his bags and kissed his wife
And then set off for Bruges.

And hardly was he out the door
When up popped sneaky John
To carry out the next sly part
Of his almighty con.

Dressed in his Sunday best he said
'Well now' to the wife,
All his emotions were on fire,
His lust was running rife.

So I'll not beat about the bush,
I'll lay it out – and straight,
He gave the wife the hundred francs
And then became her 'mate'.

And that whole long, tumultuous night,
Well they enjoyed their fun,
And in the morning when he left
He gave to everyone

A kindly smile, a cheery wave
And no-one there suspected
To what the merchant's wife that night
Had blithely been subjected.

He left the house – the merchant then
Made his fraught return,
Upon his countenance he wore
A look of grave concern.

He told his wife, 'My merchandise
Cost me a whole lot more
Than all the money spirited
Upstairs within my store.

'I need to borrow quite a sum –
Like twenty thousand crowns,
But do not worry, this is just
Commerce's ups and downs.

'And so I'll ride to Paris on
The morrow – with all speed
And in a trice I'll sort it out
And borrow what I need.

'But before I go, I think
I'll pass the time of day
With dear friend John and check out what
The good man has to say.'

And so the two old friends met up
To have a pleasant word,
The merchant told the sneaky Monk
About what had occurred.

He said, 'My merchandise all cost
A lot more than I thought,
And now I find I'm in a fix –
My money's running short.

'So off to Paris I must go,'
He said with muffled groan.
'A sum of twenty thousand crowns
I need now as a loan.'

John the Monk then gasped aloud
Pretending to look glum.
He said, 'Upon my word dear chap
That is a tidy sum.

'And if I had it be assured
I'd lend it all, you'd see,
You were so kind when you forked out
That timely loan for me.'

And then you won't believe what he
Just boldly up and said –
Such cheek as his just takes your breath
And makes you shake your head.

For as we know he used the cash
To bribe the merchant's wife
To let him have his wicked way
To liven up his life.

And now he told the merchant this,
All bold and unafraid,
'I gave your wife the hundred francs
And so the loan's repaid.

'She will confirm this I am sure,
She placed it in your box.'
Well have you ever come across
A more sly, cunning fox.

And then he said with jaunty wave,
'Well thanks a lot my friend,
The loan was handy, it ensured
That I achieved my end.

'And now I really must be off,
The Abbot waits for me,
Give my best wishes to your wife
And God's peace be with thee.'

The merchant went to see his wife
And his dear spouse he kissed,
And then again – until she cried,
'Good husband, please desist.'

The merchant though was undeterred
By this abrupt rebuff
He tried again but then she said,
'By heavens, that's enough!'

So then the merchant looked at her
Now slightly at a loss,
And said, 'You know my dearest wife
You've made me somewhat cross.

'For John before he left gave me
His earnest, grateful thanks
For a loan I'd given him
Which was a hundred francs.

'And then he said he'd given you
All of this money back,
And so my dear, do tell me please
Why have you been so slack.

'You should have told me right away
The loan had been repaid.'
The wife saw then immediately
How John's plan had been laid.

She tossed her hair and flashed her eyes
And made her face look sweet,
And then began to speak and she
Was nimble on her feet.

She said, 'It's true that dear friend John
Gave all the cash to me
Which I thought was a gift so I
Could make myself to be

'A lovely, smart and well-dressed wife
Of whom you would be proud,
A wife that caused the heads to turn
When walking in a crowd.

'I thought he gave the cash to prove
His friendship was sublime,
For not a moment did I think
'Twas your cash all the time.

'And now I've spent it on fine clothes.'
(She thought, 'That John is spiteful.')
'My only motivation dear
Was so I'd look delightful.

'And now I am in debt to you
But this much do I say,
You've other debtors worse than me
Who're very slow to pay.

'But I'm your wife, so husband dear,'
And then she smiled and said,
'Just put it on my tally and
I'll pay it back in bed.

'And so good husband cheer up now,
Forgive my little sin.'
The merchant gazed upon his wife
And then began to grin.

'Well all right,' he said, 'but now
My darling please attend,
In future be more careful and
Just watch how much you spend!'

'Dear Lady Prioress, sweet ma'am.'

THE PRIORESS'S PROLOGUE

'Well done by Corpus Dominus,'
Cried our exultant Host.
'Good Shipman that was such a tale
So to your health I toast.

'And to you fellows gathered here
I give you this advice,
Don't let a Monk pass through your door.
No, not at any price.

'Keep them from your wives – for you
Can see what they're about.
Yes, shut your door and firmly too
And keep the rascals out.

'It must be clear to everyone
That they're all over-sexed.'
Then turning to the company,
He said, 'So who'll be next?'

And then he said respectfully
All hesitant and shy,
With such politeness in his voice
And with a nervous sigh,

'Dear Lady Prioress, sweet ma'am,
If you are of a mind,
If you don't feel averse to it,
If you would be so kind,

'If you are not too tired and if
It's what you wish to do,
If you are of a mind to speak
And really fancy to,

'Then dear Lady will you now,
If it won't put you out,
Tell us a tale which as it's you
Is sure to be devout?'

The Prioress demurely said,
'I'll gladly tell a story,
But good Host I am inclined
To tell one that's quite gory.

'But it's uplifting in its way,
Though also very sad,
It's all about a little boy,
A quite amazing lad.'

The villain lurked in shadows as
He saw the boy advance

THE PRIORESS'S TALE

Within an Asian city once
There stood a little school,
A Christian place where children learnt
Life's each and every rule.

They learnt how they should all behave
And how to sing and read,
The teachers there attended to
Each child's specific need.

But most of all the teachers taught
How sinners should forgive
And cherish others – thus they showed
The Christian way to live.

Now in this school, a little boy
Studied hard each day,
He was a pleasant youngster and
He had a bookish way.

His mother was a widow,
Her husband was in heaven,
And all she had in all the world
Was her sweet lad of seven.

He learnt his lessons well and when
He saw the image there
Of Mary, our Lord's mother – well,
He knelt in fervent prayer.

But then one day whilst hard at work
This little youngster heard
Some children singing – he became
Entranced by every word.

They sang '*Alma redemptoris*'
It stirred his very soul –
To learn it from that moment on
Became the young lad's goal.

He begged another lad at school
To tell him what it meant.
'It's Latin!' sniffed the older boy,
'For this I have no bent.'

But still he said he'd have a go
And told the little lad
That when translated all these words
Gave tidings – oh so glad.

'It says the Virgin Mary is
All goodness and close by,
So bow to her and she'll take care
Of your soul when you die.'

The little boy was overcome
With reverence and joy.
Nobody loved Christ's mother like
That seven-year-old boy.

He said, 'I mean to learn this hymn
Before next Christmas-tide.'
And he was true unto his word
For how that young lad tried.

He memorized it word for word
And then he learnt to sing
The whole of it quite beautifully
And with a tuneful ring.

And every day he'd sing it twice
And normally his rule
Was to sing it while he walked
To and fro from school.

One final most endearing thing
I must now quickly add,
Sweet Mary filled his heart, he was,
A most besotted lad.

She filled his every waking hour,
He saw her as his guide,
And every moment of the day
He thought her by his side.

And so he'd sing his hymn around
The town both far and wide,
His love of it and Mary too
Was something he'd not hide.

But others who were living there
Thought his singing wrong,
They didn't like the sentiments
Expressed within the song.

He'd sing, '*Alma redemptoris*'
And this would make them mad,
So some of them made up their minds
To kill the poor sweet lad.

A foul assassin then was hired
To do their dirty work,
A man who from all fiendish acts
Was never known to shirk.

This awful murderer, this beast
Then set about his task.
What did he do, what was his plan?
My friends, you may well ask.

It makes me tremble here to tell
Of his foul, cruel deed,
Of how he grabbed that innocent
And caused him thus to bleed.

The lad was walking down a street
Singing out the chorus
Of his song, he sang with glee,
'*Alma redemptoris*'.

The villain lurked in shadows as
He saw the boy advance,
He grabbed him from behind – the boy
Just didn't stand a chance.

He held his arms and with a knife
He cut the sweet lad's throat,
His blood poured down in torrents on
His little overcoat.

And then this ghoul from hell did throw
The poor lad in a pit,
And there he lay, his arms outstretched
Quite pale – with his throat slit.

Then came the time his mother thought
He should be home from school,
He never came – she did her best
To stay both calm and cool.

But worry turned to anger – then
Blind panic gripped her soul,
She tried all night to keep her fears
In check and in control.

When daylight came at last, she went
In search of her dear child,
She was a-feared but little thought
Of how he'd been defiled.

Throughout the town the widow searched,
Fraught with anxiety,
What had become of her sweet boy?
Wherever could he be?

Sick with worry – overwhelmed,
With panic of a kind
Not difficult to comprehend –
She almost lost her mind.

She searched and searched – where could he be?
Her mind, she wracked and wracked,
Till finally by chance she stood
Right where he'd been attacked.

She asked the folk all gathered round,
'Have you seen my dear son?'
They shook their heads and lied and said
They'd not seen anyone.

But then – was it Christ's mother made
The widow cry out loud?
For she called out her poor son's name
Despite the hostile crowd.

Was it just chance that as she called
She happened to be near
The filthy pit, which held entombed
The son she held so dear?

Then as she called – I swear to you
The most amazing thing,
A voice rang out with clear soft notes
And such distinctive ring.

'*O Alma redemptoris*'
To tell it brings a tear,
For though his throat was cut and bled
He sang out loud and clear.

And people came from everywhere
To wonder at it all
For was there ever such a thing
With power to enthral?

With lamentations – disbelief,
They took him from that hole,
And every decent person there
Prayed for the sweet lad's soul.

They placed him on a funeral bier
And still he kept on singing,
They took him to the abbey where
The abbey bell was ringing.

And everybody there that day
Was shaken to the core,
And his poor, desperate mother then
Just fainted on the floor.

She fell beside her poor son's bier –
Nobody could console
This mother now quite desolate –
A sad and broken soul.

Meanwhile all those entangled in
The killing of the lad
Were rounded up and paid the price
For this foul deed – so bad.

For they were told they'd have to die –
This was what they deserved,
And soon the town's stern magistrate
Ensured this was observed.

For that same day they had strong ropes
Placed around their throats,
And sentence was then carried out
Just as the law denotes.

But back now to the abbey where
The innocent still lies
Amid the wailing of the crowd
And his poor mother's cries.

He lies there now so silently
And they intend to place
His stricken body in a grave
Where he can lie in grace.

And so the Abbot steps up to
This lad who lies alone,
A little boy so badly used
With throat cut to the bone.

The congregation bow their heads
And silence reigns supreme,
And everybody wishes that
This scene was but a dream.

They sprinkle holy water on
That little body there,
They do it with solemnity
Accompanied by a prayer.

The water trickles on the boy
And then – upon my word,
A voice broke out across the crowd –
The sweetest ever heard.

For as the water touched the boy
They heard that soulful chorus,
It filled the abbey, brought a tear –
'*O Alma redemptoris.*'

The people gathered there all gasped
For they were struck with awe
By this pure singing – by this boy –
By everything they saw.

The holy Abbot was a man
Of piety and calm,
He asked the boy, 'How can you sing
When you have suffered harm?

'How can you sing with purity
That reaches to the sky
To move the very heart of God
Who sits with grace on high?

'For your poor throat is cut right through.
In truth, you should be dead.'
The little boy lay pale and still
And this is what he said.

'It's true my throat is severed through,
By rights I should have died
But our dear Saviour, Christ the Lord
Was ever by my side.

'And his dear mother seemed to come
And speak to me and say,
"Although you're dead, you must still sing
'*O Alma*' every day.

"It isn't right that you should die,
Somebody quite so young."
And then she placed a shiny pearl
Upon my outstretched tongue.

'She said, "While this sweet, precious pearl
Remains quite safely here
You'll sing for all the world but if
The pearl should disappear,

"Or if it should be taken from
Your tongue and cast away
That is the time I'll come for you,
I'll come that very day.

"So do not be distressed for if
This pearl is ever taken
I'll care for you, my dear sweet boy
You'll never be forsaken." '

The Abbot then, in kindly way
Looked at the boy so young
And gently, with humility
He touched the young lad's tongue.

He held it for a moment and
You've never seen so much
Tenderness and sadness in
A simple, caring touch.

And then he gently took the pearl
And clasped his hands to pray,
Till mercifully the stricken boy
Passed peacefully away.

The tears upon the Abbot's face
Were torturous to see,
They fell like rain – he dropped then to
The ground upon one knee.

And then he fell across the floor,
And there he lay quite prone,
Wracked with appalling sorrow he
Just lay there like a stone.

He knew he'd seen a miracle
As did the congregation,
And everybody gathered there
Prayed for their own salvation.

Then finally they rose and took
The little boy away,
They placed him in a sepulchre
Safe from the light of day.

And there he lies – enclosed, entombed –
And this I must now say
I think that everybody here
Will humbly wish to pray

That God grant us the fortitude
To show our sins defeat,
And that we go to heaven where
This little boy we'll meet.

He came across a giant who
Stood growling by his den

CHAUCER TRIES TO TELL HIS TALE OF SIR TOPAZ

The silence that fell all about
Now that the Prioress
Had finished her distressing tale –
Had finished her address

Was something quite incredible,
Quite wondrous to behold,
And everybody bowed their head
In awe at what she'd told.

It was a melancholy mood
That had now been installed
For everybody there that day
Was mesmerised – enthralled.

The all-pervading silence then
Was heavy – reeked of gloom,
But it was broken by a sound –
A loud and raucous boom.

It was our Host and once again
He laughed and cracked a joke,
And in a tick he'd changed the mood
And cheered up all the folk.

And then he turned to me and said,
'So Chaucer, tell me do
What thoughts pass through your mind my friend.
What kind of chap are you?

'Now everybody clear a path,
Please let our good friend through.
Perhaps he has a tale to tell
Which has a kinder hue.

'Come forward sir – it's your turn now,
Step up and please make haste,
Though I can see that just like me
You have an ample waist.

'But don't you fret, for it's no sin
To be so wide of hip,
The ladies like it as it gives
Something that's firm to grip.

'Now dear friend Chaucer, hear me please,
I beg on the behalf
Of all your new friends gathered here,
For God's sake – make us laugh!

'We've had our fill of sadness now,
So please good chap regale
The company with something bright –
Please tell a happy tale.'

I felt embarrassed but replied,
(For I'd not be outdone)
'I'll do my best, and hope you'll think
That it's a worthy one.

'So if you all are quite prepared
To give to me your time
I'll tell my little tale which is
An old one and in rhyme.'

The Host clasped both his hands with glee,
He cried, 'Well spoken man,
I'm sure that you can tell a tale
If anybody can.

'You have a certain way – an air
Of clever competence,
And so dear Chaucer if you please,
I beg you to commence.'

And so I then began my tale,
One that I felt for sure
Would entertain – I was intent
That I'd not be a bore.

It concerned a merry knight,
Sir Topaz was his name,
He was courageous in his way
And so enjoyed some fame.

His face was pale like baker's dough,
He had a handsome nose,
He wore a most expensive gown
Along with Belgian hose.

He liked to hunt and always had
A goshawk on his wrist,
And many were his chances for
A secret lover's tryst.

For lots of ladies fancied him,
But Topaz, brave and bold
Would never let a sweet girl's love
Ensnare him or take hold.

For he was not the lustful kind
But of a noble turn,
So ladies had to let their love
Just unrequited burn.

Then one day Sir Topaz rode
Upon his fine grey steed,
With lance in hand, his sword well sheathed –
A stirring sight indeed.

Through a forest, lush and green
He rode the whole long day,
Admiring all the wildlife there
As he went on his way.

But later on the Knight grew tired,
He thought he'd have a sleep,
And there within that woodland glade
He had a sleep so deep

That when he woke ensconced within
That peaceful, lovely scene,
He cried, 'Oh what a dream I've had
About a Fairy Queen.

'She was so beautiful – I vow
That she was far above
All other women that I've seen –
It's she that I must love.'

Poor old Sir Topaz worked himself
Into a right old state.
He cried, 'This Fairy Queen alone
Is fit to be my mate.'

And then he jumped back on his horse
To search throughout the land,
To find the Fairy Queen – then win
That lovely maiden's hand.

Through valleys wide and mountains high
Our good Knight travelled – then
He came across a giant who
Stood growling by his den.

He snarled, 'I am Sir Elephant,
I'm dangerous and mean,
And I live here and I protect
The lovely Fairy Queen.

'If you don't go away I'll wipe
That smile right off your face.'
And then he swung around his head
A fearsome-looking mace.

Sir Topaz had no armour there,
So, fearful of attack,
He turned upon his tail but said,
'Good sir, I will be back.'

He made his way towards a town
And on arrival there,
He went into a cosy inn
And there pulled up a chair.

He called for wine, the very best
To give himself a treat,
And tasty dishes, finely cooked
And then began to eat...

'For heavens sake, no more, I say.
Oh give us all a break.'
It was our Host and he cried out,
'No more for mercy's sake.

'In all my life I've never heard
Such rubbish or such talk,
I tell you Chaucer, this daft road
Is one I just won't walk.

'I've never heard such nonsense or
Such drivel anywhere,
It really is atrocious stuff,
It is too much to bear.

'For as you got into your stride
The whole thing just got worse,
And I must say I've never known
Such downright awful verse.

'I guess they call it doggerel
But it's not worth a turd,
I tell you sir, it's quite the worst
That I have ever heard.'

Well this was pretty hurtful stuff
But I don't like a quarrel,
I think they're quite undignified,
Time-wasting and immoral.

And so I kept myself composed
And gave a little grin
Determined that I'd stay quite calm
And take it on the chin.

Our Host then said most thoughtfully
While stroking his fat nose,
'Now Chaucer, my dear friend, why not
Tell us a tale in prose.'

I gladly said I would and told
My tale of Melibee,
It is a serious debate
So let's just let it be.

I won't include it here my friends,
I wish to keep this light,
But when I told the company
They thought it was all right.

'Dear Host, I'll do my best.'

THE NUN'S PRIEST'S PROLOGUE

Our Host reined in his horse and said
To our good friend, the Priest,
'It's your turn now – you'll not be last
And therefore won't be least.

'So tell a tale to cheer us up
As we all travel on.
A funny tale, a happy tale.
Step forward, dear Sir John.'

And so that ever pleasant man,
Sir John who had been blest
With kindly manner – smiled and said,
'Dear Host, I'll do my best.'

Oh my, oh my, how he did cluck

THE NUN'S PRIEST'S TALE

Long years ago, the Lord knows when –
In a cottage by
A meadow in the countryside,
Beneath the English sky,

There dwelt a widow, old and poor,
For her life was quite tough
But somehow she still made her way,
God sent her just enough.

Her daughters lived there with her too,
They led a frugal life,
And it had been that way since when
She'd ceased to be a wife.

No fancy food would ever find
Its way onto her board,
But she did not complain for she
Was thankful to the Lord.

She blessed Him for what came her way.
She never would complain,
For faith and prayers would see her through
And they would help sustain

This good and noble woman but
Now that you've taken stock
Of her poor life – I must confess –
This tale's about a cock;

For in her yard she kept this cock,
So fine and cavalier.
Extremely proud – he ruled the roost.
His name was Chanticleer.

Now when it came to crowing – well,
This cockerel could claim
To really stand alone and so
In those parts, his great fame

Was heralded by everyone,
For every single morn
They'd hear him crowing boisterously
To welcome in the dawn.

And it was said, no other cock
Could sing with voice so clear,
Or with such punctuality
As good old Chanticleer.

And what a sight he surely was
Most handsome and so bold,
There really is no doubt that he
Was something to behold.

With comb of quite the deepest red
And feathers brash and bright
Of gold and green and burnished hue,
Oh he was quite a sight.

And living with him in the yard,
Old Chanticleer was blessed
With seven hens who all were there,
(As I am sure you've guessed),

To pleasure him, for they were his
Own harem – lucky lad.
So overall it could be said
His life was not too bad.

Amongst these clucking hens there was
One of especial note,
So kind of nature, she was called
The damsel, Pertelote.

She was a lovely looking hen
And also very smart.
And Chanticleer, since she'd arrived
Had given her his heart.

So she could wind him round her claw
And make him do her whim,
And when she asked a favour – this
Was just sheer bliss to him.

Now one day Chanticleer dozed off
Upon his favourite perch
With Pertelote beside him there –
Then he began to lurch,

From side to side he swayed around.
He groaned, he moaned, he cried.
He carried on in such a way
You'd think someone had died.

The damsel Pertelote cried out,
'My precious heart, what's wrong?
Wake up!' And then poor Chanticleer,
He nearly fell headlong

From off his perch, but he awoke
Just in the nick of time.
Another moment, he'd have been
Down in the muck and grime.

Recovering he then cried out,
'Oh, Pertelote, my dear,
I've had the most horrendous dream.'
And then poor Chanticleer,

Began to shake and then he said,
'You really can't conceive
How horrible the whole thing was,
I swear I did perceive

'Within this dream, an awful cur,
A beast of rusty red,
And in his heart, he had one thought,
That was to see me dead.'

And so that once proud cockerel,
That yard king, Chanticleer,
Quaked with overpowering fright,
He trembled there with fear.

Well, Pertelote looked at the cock,
At her once favoured beau,
Then turned her head disdainfully,
She didn't want to know.

And then in mocking tone she spoke.
She made it very clear
She'd changed her high opinion of
Her once dear Chanticleer.

'I never ever thought to see
Such cowardice from you.
I cannot love a spineless fool
No matter what I do.

'I loved you once but I declare
You timorous upstart,
I cannot love a cock like you,
You've forfeited my heart.

'You've lost my very high regard.
You've dropped in my esteem,
For how can you behave as though
You're frightened by a dream.

'You cannot be a proper cock
To act like this – I swear
That dreams are purely in the mind,
A fancy in the air.'

And so began a great debate
Twixt this unhappy pair,
On dreams and what they really meant,
And should all fowl beware,

For were dreams there to warn them
Of some impending doom,
And if a hen or cockerel
Should have one steeped in gloom,

Did this then mean it would come true?
Was it a warning sign?
Did dreams and stark reality
In some way thus combine?

Oh, how these two philosophers
Debated dreams that day,
Till lovelorn Chanticleer declared,
'Well, darling, come what may,

'When I'm asleep upon this perch,
With you dear, by my side,
Well, I am just filled up with love
And all-consuming pride,

'Just knowing you are close to me
Is bliss – or so it seems,
It causes me to mock such thoughts
And makes me scorn all dreams.'

And then proud Chanticleer flew off
With fluttering of wings
He left his perch – his mind now free
Of all those scary things.

Once more he strutted round the yard,
And each and every hen
Paid court to him – once more he was
King of the chicken pen.

With head held high he strode around,
Why, just like royalty,
As if to say to everyone,
'I beg you, look at me.

'For surely I'm the finest bird.
Yes, quite the finest cock
That you have ever seen – so friends
Come hither and take stock.'

And when he found a grain of seed
Somewhere upon the ground,
He'd hold it in his handsome beak
And make a clucking sound.

And all his hens would quickly come
And Chanticleer would then
Most graciously bestow the seed
Upon his favoured hen.

But while all this was going on,
While Chanticleer was there
Carrying on like royalty –
His head held in the air,

Great danger was then lurking,
Unhappily close by,
For out beyond the little yard
A crafty fox did lie.

He'd watched the hens and Chanticleer
For many a long day,
With cold, sharp eyes and cunning mind,
Intent to find a way

Of having one for his next meal.
And who had most to fear?
Why, that proud, prancing, boastful chap,
That bighead, Chanticleer.

The fox's piercing eyes fell on
A lush, green cabbage patch.
He slowly inched his way with care,
Determined now to catch,

Poor Chanticleer who rested there –
And as that fox did steal
Upon the unsuspecting cock,
He thought, 'Oh, what a meal!

'That tubby cock will be a treat.'
His mouth began to drool.
And all the time old Chanticleer,
That unsuspecting fool,

Sat motionless – he took the sun
Until he cast his eye
Towards the very self-same spot
On which the fox did lie.

Oh my, oh my, how he did cluck
And kick up such a storm
When fearful Chanticleer espied
The fox's slinking form.

Though Chanticleer had never seen
A fox before – he thought,
'It wouldn't be that good for me
If I was ever caught

'By such a scary creature.'
So fear began to ooze
From every pore – he was convinced
The fox was real bad news.

His every instinct was to flee.
Find safety right away,
But then the fox said pleasantly,
'Let's pass the time of day.

'You have no cause to be a-feared.
Please do not be alarmed.
There is no way that I would want
To ever see you harmed.

'So please believe me when I say
I wish to be your friend.
I only want to lie right here
And quietly attend

'While you sing all your lovely songs.
Oh, what a treat to hear
Your singing which is so divine,
It's heaven to the ear.

'I used to hear your father sing
And what a voice he had,
But truthfully he couldn't sing
As well as you, my lad.

'Your voice is quite extraordinary.
So round and full and whole.
It stokes emotions deep inside
And stirs one's very soul.'

Well flattery is powerful stuff.
It turns the mind and then
Makes fools of its recipients,
It ruins sober men.

It's something merely to be smelt,
Not swallowed down piecemeal,
So Chanticleer was fool indeed
To heed the fox's spiel.

But sad to say, he fell for it,
For he was no great thinker.
He took the bait and with it too
The hook, the line and sinker.

For he stood upright on his toes,
He stretched his neck so high,
He closed his eyes, he took a breath,
Then let some sweet notes fly.

But hardly had a soaring note
Left Chanticleer's voice box
Than he was pounced upon and by
That very sneaky fox.

His jaws closed on the cockerel's throat
And snapped shut like a snare.
Poor Chanticleer was gripped with fear
And desperate despair.

The fox flung Chanticleer across
His strong and brawny back.
He carried him with gross disdain
As though he were a sack.

Now you could say that Chanticleer
Who'd fallen for this bluff
Had got his just deserts for all
His strutting and such stuff.

But even so, it would be hard
If this turned out to be
The end of such a fine, bold cock
Who'd always been carefree.

Well, happily help was at hand –
The widow acted guard
For all the creatures in her care,
So rushed into the yard.

Her daughters followed after her.
'Oh look,' they cried as one.
'Look what that awful, sneaky fox
Has just now gone and done.

'He's got our darling Chanticleer.
He's got him by the throat.
Oh dear, he'll never ever now
Sing out another note.'

'I'll not have this,' the widow cried.
'Come on for if we're quick,
We'll catch him and save Chanticleer.'
And then she grabbed a stick.

She yelled out to her neighbours there
And to her dogs and then
They all set off, a seething crowd
Of women, dogs and men.

They waved their fists and cursed that fox
And chased with all their might.
It must be said that sly, old fox
Had never felt such fright.

He ran as fast as fox's can
But still the people came.
They called him every awful thing,
Their anger now aflame.

Poor Chanticleer lay on his back
And though still in great shock
He started coming round a bit,
Then started taking stock.

And then a very cunning thought
Across his mind did steal,
It just might save him from the fate
Of being fox's meal.

He gave a little croak and then
He said, 'If I were you
Caught in a spot like this, good fox,
I know what I would do.

'I'd turn around and face this crowd.
How dare they treat you thus.
Hounding you in such a way
And causing all this fuss.

'It's disrespectful to a fox
And one so debonair.
If I were you I'd bare my teeth
And give them all a scare.'

The fox thought he was safe, for now
He'd reached a leafy wood.
And so he thought, 'What this cock says
Sounds sensible and good.'

And so he cried, 'It's what I'll do.'
But as he thus did speak,
It caused his jaws to open wide
And with a joyful shriek,

Our Chanticleer flew off at speed
Up into the trees.
'Oh what a crafty trick,' he thought.
'Oh what a clever wheeze.'

The fox looked up unhappily
For there sat his next dinner,
But he still thought he could succeed
And still come out the winner.

'Oh my dear friend,' he slyly said,
'Did I hold you too tight?
I'm sorry for I did not mean
To give you such a fright.

'So come on down and speak to me
And then I can explain
Just what I had in mind, I'll not
Cause you distress again.'

The cock looked down from up the tree.
'You must be joking, fox.
It's but a fool that doesn't heed
The lessons from life's knocks.

'You'll fool me once but never twice
For that would surely make
A simpleton of me – I'm not
A dunce, for heavens sake.'

At this point then, the Priest did smile
And faced the company.
He said, 'So that's my little tale,
From which, I trust you'll see

'It has a moral which I feel
Rings very loud and clear,
And that's to blank out flatterers
Whenever they draw near.

'And if you think this tale of mine
Is really quite absurd,
And falls into the category
Of "daftest ever heard"

'Well, just take note of what it tells,
The moral there within,
And so I say, God keep you safe
And save you all from sin.'

The good Physician raised his hand
And said, 'I'll have a go.'

EPILOGUE TO THE NUN'S PRIEST'S TALE

When the Priest had told his tale
The company did cheer,
And our good Host remarked, 'Such fun,
That tale of Chanticleer.

'And what a moral to the tale
Right there at the end,
One I'm sure we'll heed – and well –
So thank you kindly friend.'

And then our merry Host did cast
His twinkling eye around
And said, 'So who will now step up
To keep us all spellbound?'

The good Physician raised his hand
And said, 'I'll have a go.
I'll tell a tale I dearly hope
That none of you will know.'

He looked as they strolled by

THE PHYSICIAN'S TALE

There is an ancient tale that's told
About a famous knight,
Virginius was his name and he
Was rich and did all right.

He had a wife and daughter too –
This daughter was so fair,
With ruby lips and sparkling eyes,
Soft skin and silken hair.

When Nature formed her she'd been kind,
This girl was nothing less,
Than really quite adorable,
Just like a sweet princess.

She had the kind of figure
To turn just any head,
And every little thing she did
Confirmed she was well bred.

Of course she was most virtuous,
A virgin still for sure,
So innocent and undefiled,
Quite perfect to the core.

So now you've got a picture
Of this elegant female,
I can with confidence relate
My lust-filled, sorry tale.

It starts upon one pleasant morn
When dressed in her best gown,
The daughter with her mother dear
Set out to go to town.

And on arrival as they walked
Along a cobbled street
It was their great misfortune there
A haughty judge to meet.

This judge held power o'er many things
Of small moment and large,
It seemed that everything in town
Came under this man's charge.

And as they passed this pompous judge,
He looked as they strolled by,
And saw the girl's fine beauty with
His selfish, lustful eye.

268

'Oh what a comely lass she is.
Oh what a girl,' he thought.
And in a flash I think we see
The end that he now sought.

'I'll have my wicked way with her,
With this sweet lass I'll lay.
Somehow I'll make this fine girl mine,
I'll have her, come what may.'

And so I think it's fair to say
The devil entered him
For he was now determined that
He'd satisfy his whim.

But he knew that the girl was pure,
Not up for sinful play.
Flowery words would not persuade,
Whatever he might say.

He also knew there was no chance
She'd ever take a fee,
And so he sought with care to find
Just what his course should be.

And then a really nasty thought
Suddenly occurred.
That wicked judge just smiled and then
He quickly sent out word

For a shameless ne'er-do-well
To come to him that day,
And then he outlined his base plan
For which he said he'd pay.

He made the blackguard swear with force
He'd never tell a soul
Of what the judge was up to and
Of his unworthy goal.

He said, 'If you divulge my scheme
I'll see you are disgraced,
And with my powers I'll see your head
Upon a block is placed.'

The man called Claudius just shrugged
And said, with not a frown,
'Don't worry judge, I'm up for it
And I won't let you down.'

And so a day or two passed by
And then this bent judge sought
To put his devious scheme in place,
So took his seat in court.

Then as he sat bewigged and robed
All proud and noble there,
And looking down to thus imply
That all he did was fair,

There came into the courtroom then,
The evil man we know,
And as he entered, with respect
This lying snake bowed low.

He said, 'My name is Claudius.
I come to plead my cause,
And hope you grant me justice by
Applying our sound laws.

'I make complaint against a man,
Virginius by name.
Skulduggery and falsehood too
Have been his claim to fame.

'He holds a servant girl who he
Claims is his daughter fair.
His insolence is quite grotesque –
However can he dare.

'For she was stolen from me
When she was very young
And now he says she is his girl
But speaks with crooked tongue.'

The judge said, 'Call Virginius.
Tell him to come to court,
And then with careful questioning
This matter I will sort.'

When poor Virginius arrived
He stood there truly shocked,
His protestations of the truth
Were just dismissed and mocked.

He said, 'She is my daughter.'
You should have heard his cries.
'This man is just a bounder, judge.
He speaks a pack of lies.'

Of course the judge was not intent
On being fair or just,
His overriding aim was now
To satisfy his lust.

Putting on his gravest face,
So stern, severe and black,
He said, 'My ruling's final –
She must be given back.

'For she was clearly stolen
All those years ago.'
Though Virginius tried to plead
He didn't want to know.

He wouldn't heed the poor man's cries.
He just ignored his pleas.
Virginius clasped his hands and then
Sank down upon his knees.

'She is my own dear daughter
Nurtured from a child.'
The judge looked down with anger now –
With flashing eyes so wild.

'Bring the young maid to my court.'
(Oh what a dreadful threat.)
'She must be handed to this man.
My judgement is now set.'

Virginius saw at once just what
Was really going on,
He saw the courtroom drama
Was just a devious con.

He saw that this was not about
Doing what was just,
No – it was all to satisfy
The judge's selfish lust.

Poor Virginius left the court
His mind in disarray,
Emotions all aflame he now
Made his fraught, desperate way

Back home to see his daughter who
Was sewing blithely there,
Of all the goings on in court
Completely unaware.

Her father called her to his side
And drawing in his breath,
He said, 'You have to choose my dear
Between great shame or death.'

The poor man told her everything.
He said, 'Light of my life,
To think you must be shamed this way
Or die upon my knife.

'My belief is you must die.'
(He was in such a state.)
'I say this out of fervent love
And not at all from hate.

'For when you die, I die as well,
For never will I see
Another happy day – your death
Will be the death of me.

'For your despairing father must
Strike off your head,' he said.
'I couldn't bear the shame they plan
And so must see you dead.'

'Oh father dear,' the sweet girl cried.
'Must I really die?
Is there no way we can refute
This base, unworthy lie?'

She flung her arms around his neck,
Her tears fell like spring rain.
She cried, she hugged him desperately
And then cried out again.

'Am I to die while still so young?
Is this the end of me?'
Her father hugged her close and sighed,
'There is no remedy.'

'Then give me just a little time
To contemplate my end,
For you would do this for a foe –
A person not your friend.'

Virginius bowed his weary head,
Emotions all a-spin.
It was so dreadful, for the maid
Was quite devoid of sin.

The sweet, young girl then swooned away
But not for very long,
She soon came round and then declared,
'Dear father, I'll be strong.

'I bless the Lord, for I will die
A chaste and decent maid.
And I choose death o'er morbid shame,
So father – with your aid

'I will depart this fiendish world
That treats this poor girl ill,
Thus father, take your sword and then
In God's name – do your will.

'Cut off my head, but father dear,
Please do it gently, pray.'
And with these sweet, courageous words
Once more she swooned away.

Her father stood there quite borne down
With anguish of a kind
That truly in this whole wide world
Is very hard to find.

She was his darling little girl –
That it should come to this.
He leant across her one last time,
Bestowed a silent kiss.

Then he who'd helped to give her life
Prayed quickly to the Lord,
And then with heavy breaking heart
The father took his sword.

While she lay there so silently,
Before the poor girl woke
He raised his sword and struck her neck
With one almighty stroke.

Her head fell from her shoulders,
Her blood was everywhere.
He lifted up his daughter's head
By her long, golden hair,

And then he carried it to court –
The judge was sitting still.
'Here is my daughter's head,' he cried,
'A victim of your will.

'She died to save herself from shame.'
He spoke with sheer disgust.
'It was the only way that she
Could overcome your lust.

'For it was clear to everyone
The nature of your game.
If you had any decency
You'd hang your head in shame.'

The judge could see he had no choice,
Silence the father – or
It would be he the judge who'd be
Accounting to the law.

He called out to his band of men,
'This villain must now die,
For he has come into this court
And told a monstrous lie.

'Take him outside and tie him up,
Then hang him from a tree,
And let him swing until he's dead –
This is the court's decree.'

Well, this was pretty heavy stuff
Which many thought unfair,
They knew the judge was quite inclined
To have the odd affair.

They knew about his roving eye
And of his lustful manner,
So now they thought, into his works
They'd throw the people's spanner.

They all rose up as one great force,
Determined to prevail,
And thus it was, the judge was seized
And then thrown into jail.

Into that prison where he'd sent
Many a wretched soul,
And now he languished there within
That very self-same hole.

He felt distraught that everyone
Knew just how much he'd lied
And so one day, distressed, he then
Committed suicide.

As for Claudius, he escaped
From being hung – for he
(Some said without good reason)
Was granted clemency.

Virginius he did plead for him
And said, 'Exile the rogue.'
And as this form of punishment
Was at that time in vogue,

Claudius was sent away.
He was a lucky lad!
It was a very close escape
The evil scoundrel had.

'And so I say to one and all,'
The good Physician said,
'The Lord takes full account of just
The type of life you've led.

'And whether you be lowly born
Or noble and discerning,
Or lacking education or
Someone of great learning,

'You never know when God will smite
And cast the sinner down,
It makes no difference if you wear
A beggar's cap or crown.

'And so my message here today
That I give you for nowt,
Is give up sinning now, before
Your sins all find you out.'

'I think I'll have a drink.'

EPILOGUE TO THE PHYSICIAN'S TALE

Well, once he'd finished what a noise,
Our Host cried out aloud.
'God's nails and blood, oh what a tale.
Quite awful,' he avowed.

'Alas, that sweet, forsaken maid,
To lose her life that way.
And that cold, sneaky, evil judge!'
He shouted in dismay.

One thing you truly must admit
Our Host, he lived each tale.
It stirred his soul, it lit his fuse,
It riled him without fail.

'Death to dishonest lawyers.
A plague on every one.'
There was no stopping his tirade
Now that it had begun.

'They should be watched with care,' he yelled.
'And when they let you down,
Sent into prison there to rot
Or run right out of town.

'Oh that poor girl who died that way.
To lose her lovely head.
Still makes no difference how she died,
For being dead is dead.

'In truth her beauty caused her fall,
It's scary, is it not,
That often what seems like a gift
Can land us in a spot.

'For Mother Nature had endowed
This maiden with a face
As delicate and lovely as
Fine gems or soft, white lace.

'And yet this gift that Nature gave
With love as to a friend
Caused her such trouble as we saw –
It brought about her end.

'In all my life I've seldom heard
A tale so sad to hear.'
And as he spoke our gallant Host
Did wipe away a tear.

He turned to the Physician then
And said, 'I bless you sir
And all your pills and potions too,
And may they all confer

'Their healing qualities upon
All those who seek your aid,
If only they could have been used
To save that hapless maid.

'But there it is, no point at all
In getting in a state,
'Twas but a tale and truthfully
I think it was first rate.

'It touched my heart and made me feel
Such a deep emotion
I think I need a gulp or two
Of your most special potion.

'Or failing that a good strong glass
Of but the finest ale,
And then I think we all would like
A bright and cheerful tale.

'So let's stop at this welcome inn
And slake our thirst awhile,
And Pardoner will you then tell
A tale to make us smile.'

The pious pilgrims all cried out,
'Not a dirty story.
We want a tale of something good
To celebrate Christ's glory.'

The Pardoner then scratched his head
And said, 'Now let me think,
But while I thus deliberate
I think I'll have a drink!'

'And though I've no intention
To practise what I preach.'

THE PARDONER'S PROLOGUE

The Pardoner took a mighty swig
From his glass of beer,
And everybody gathered round
To make quite sure to hear

Exactly what he'd have to say.
What would his message be
And would he tell a tale to fill
The company with glee?

He said, 'Although I preach my stuff
By rote – I've learnt it well,
Of heaven and the way to see
You don't end up in hell.

'And though I freely will admit
I preach – yes, out of need,
To earn a decent living and
To satisfy my greed,

'I freely tell you one and all.'
(He supped his glass of ale).
'That though I am a hypocrite,
I still can tell a tale,

'One with a moral which is sure
To make it very plain
That there is always punishment
For all dishonest gain.

'And though I've no intention
To practise what I preach,
I bid you heed the moral that
I am about to teach.'

He finished off his ale and said,
'To drink is not a sin.
So fill my glass again good Host
And then I will begin.'

They found a bag of instant wealth –
Gold coins of the realm

THE PARDONER'S TALE

In Flanders, once upon a time
There lived three idle guys,
Who passed their time in such a way
That most folk would despise.

For they were into every vice
That's ever been invented,
When they were drunk or throwing dice,
That's when they were contented.

And they'd carouse both night and day,
They'd eat and drink too much.
They'd dance and sing and womanise
And play the lute and such.

And as they went their worthless way
They didn't give a toss,
For having fun was their desire
And wantonness was boss.

And when engrossed in their debauch
They gave no single care,
And worst of all they cursed out loud,
Oh how these three could swear.

Of women too, they had their fill,
Their morals were so loose,
That every girl they came across
They tried hard to seduce.

But now before I tell you more
Let me just say a word
About those deadly sins of which
Good people you have heard.

Take drunkenness – an awful sin,
Makes people do such things –
And not confined to common folk,
For it applies to kings.

For Herod while tanked up with wine
In drunkenness did bid
His soldiers slay the Baptist, John –
He knew not what he did.

And gluttony – a dreadful thing,
Though food seems such a treat,
You make a privy of your throat
When you do overeat.

And gambling is a sin as well.
Ignoble! Wanton! Rash!
A waste of any good man's time.
A total waste of cash.

And there is nothing worse I say
Than a gambling prince,
Enough to make a pious man
Draw back in shock and wince.

A prince who spends his time this way
Could never govern well,
If anybody's heard of one,
Then pray step up and tell.

And one last point I'll proffer,
I'd like to make it plain,
That I have little time for folk
Who naughtily profane.

For swearing is a mortal sin,
Almighty God has told
That those who curse are even worse,
Much more than thrice tenfold

Than many other sinful folk,
For this command is third
Within the ten he's handed us –
And thus he has inferred

That it is most important, friends,
And when this one was made,
God on high was adamant
That it should be obeyed.

So having made it very clear
Right at the beginning
About the pitfalls to be found
In wanton, reckless sinning,

I will continue with my tale
About these worthless types,
A feckless trio – dissolute.
All three were guttersnipes.

While other folk were hard at work
Reciting prayers and psalms,
These three lads were hard at work
A-bending their right arms.

It was the tavern where they prayed,
A worship of a sort,
For here they gulped down pints of beer
And sack and wine and port.

And rather than imbibe the Lord
They worshipped grape and grain,
And there was nothing in the world
Would make these three abstain.

Intoxicated, there they sat,
Just like naughty boys,
All slurring words and laughing loud –
But then they heard a noise.

It was the undertaker's bell
Which his young lad did wave,
To tell the world another soul
Was going to the grave.

One of the drinkers there then told
The tavern lad to go
And find out who the mourners bore
For he now wished to know.

It was through curiosity
And really nothing more.
He said, 'I want to know just who
That funeral is for.'

The tavern boy looked smug and grinned,
In fact it was a smirk.
He said, 'No need to ask, I know,
For that was old Death's work.

'Within that coffin coldly lays
Someone who was your friend,
Who but last night got deadly drunk,
Fell down and met his end.

'For that old reprobate called Death
Crept up to where he lay
And in a tick he took his life
And bore his soul away.

'Just like he's killed so many more –
So if you meet him sir
I beg you take great care for if
His wrath you do incur,

'He's just as likely to decide
To take your life as well,
And carry you to heaven or
Into the fiery hell.'

One of the young lads turned quite pale.
Another just said, 'Strewth!'
The inn's good host said to the third,
'The lad, he speaks the truth.

'Death's killed so many folk round here
Of every size and shape.
The strongest even stand no chance,
For there is no escape.'

The three debauched young men cried out
In tones both shrill and rough,
'He cannot be that hard to beat.
He's surely not that tough.

'We'll seek him out and deal with him,
Give him some of the same
As he's dealt out, we'll beat him at
The very self-same game.'

And so these three did there and then
With great resolve determine
To seek out Death, they all declared,
'We will destroy this vermin.

'He shall not have another chance
To kill another soul,
For we will kill him and we'll throw
His body in a hole.

'We'll cover it with dirt and then
'Twill put paid to the knave.
It's time that Death was buried in
A dark and dismal grave.'

And so the three all drunkenly
Declared upon their life
When they caught Death, well Death would be
Struck down – and with a knife!

So off they set upon their quest
And on the road they saw
An old man bent and weary who
Seemed poor from what he wore.

'God be with you gentlemen,'
Said he with kindly sigh.
They answered, 'Surely from your age
It's time for you to die.'

The poor old man replied and thus,
'Death doesn't want to know.
He will not take me even though
I'm ready now to go.

'I'm weary of this life, just look
At my poor wrinkled skin.
My body is just bent and bone,
Look at the state I'm in!

'If only Death would answer me
When I knock on his door
For I have had it with this life
And wish to live no more.'

But saying this the old man then
Took umbrage with the three.
'You shouldn't speak in such rough terms
When you're addressing me.

''Tis written that you show respect
To old men with no hair.'
The drunken group just laughed at him
And said, 'Old man, beware.

'For we just heard you speak about
That fellow Death and think
You are his friend and you know where
The fellow goes to drink.

'So by the holy Sacrament
You tell us all you know,
And we'll not make it hard for you,
We might just let you go.'

The old man shrugged his shoulders – he
Ignored their threats and cheek
And said, 'Go up this path right here
If it is Death you seek.

'I left him there this very day
Underneath a tree,
And if I'm right you'll find him still –
Just waiting there, you'll see.

'He's not the kind to hide away,
Not when he's work to do,
And you should find him easily,
Or maybe he'll find you!'

And so the three young reprobates
Ran off to find the tree,
And there it was, and what a sight
Was waiting there to see.

For hidden in the branches of
A quite enormous elm,
They found a bag of instant wealth –
Gold coins of the realm.

And in that instant every thought
Of Death flew out the door,
For now they had acquired such wealth
They'd search for him no more.

One of the three spoke up and said,
'Well now that we are rich
We must ensure we do things right,
We can't afford a hitch.

'If people see we have this gold
They'll think we're thieves for sure,
And they will make us answer to
The full weight of the law.

'So here's what I suggest, my friends,
Be quiet now and hark,
We'll stay right here and guard the gold
Until it's good and dark.

'And then we'll leave here furtively
And hide it well away.
So there's my plan, a good one too.
My friends, what do you say?'

The other two agreed at once
And then the first one said,
'We'll need some food and wine for we
Must be refreshed and fed.

'So I propose we now draw straws.
Who draws the longest one
Will get the job of going off
Before the day is done;

'He'll go to town to buy some fare,
So with no more ado
Let's pick a straw and see who'll go.'
And then as if on cue

He drew three straws from round his back,
Each straight and coloured brown.
The youngest drew the longest straw
So he set off for town.

As soon as he was out of sight
One of the lads did speak,
And as he spoke, his sneaky words
Of treachery did reek.

He said, 'You know I am your friend,
Truer than any other.
And as for you, I've always thought
You were just like a brother.

'Now here's a pile of gold that we
Must now divide in three,
But pause a moment for a thought
Has just occurred to me.

'There would be more to go around
If it was split in two.
If it was just divided up
Twixt your friend here and you.'

He gripped the other fellow's arm
As he so slyly spoke
To show his troubled friend that he
Was quite a decent bloke.

The other scratched his head and said,
'But how could it be done?
He knows we have the gold so he
Won't settle having none.

'What sort of yarn could we thus spin
To tie him in a knot?'
The first one said, 'Now shake my hand.
Will you agree or not?

'For I know how it can be done,
But first will you agree
To aid me in my plan and then
I'll tell the remedy?'

The scheming pair then sealed the deal.
They shook hands eagerly,
And then the first one up and said,
'Now listen carefully.

'When he comes back we'll make a joke
And here's the plan we'll hatch,
Just for some fun you'll challenge him
To have a wrestling match.

'And while you've got him thus engaged,
Arms pinned and all entwined,
I'll silently and with great stealth
Approach him from behind.

'And when he's least expecting it
I'll make a swift attack,
And with my trusty dagger here
I'll stab him in the back.

'And in the struggle you can then
Draw out your knife as well,
And then between the two of us
We'll send the lad to hell.

'And then this lovely pile of gold
So shiny, bright and nice,
Will mean the two of us can spend
Our days just playing dice.

'So this is all we have to do
Now we've agreed our pact,
And we'll be wealthy evermore
From this decisive act.'

Meanwhile the youngest went to town
To get some drink and food,
And as he made his way his thoughts
Began to change his mood.

For avarice was taking hold,
Low greed and all those things
That people of all levels feel
From common folk to kings.

'Could I find a way?' he thought,
'('Twould mean I'd needs be bold.)
To have that treasure for myself –
That lovely pile of gold.'

And then he thought, 'There is a way
To get what I desire,
I think that I can see a way
That really won't backfire.'

And so the Devil entered him,
Let fly his evil dart.
It captured first his mind and soul
And then ensnared his heart.

'I'll get some poison and then play
A sneaky, little trick.
I'll place it in the wine and then
They'll die in half a tick.'

And so he went to find a shop
That sold strong poison and
He chose a poison that was quite
The deadliest known brand.

He told the man, 'I've rats to kill.
They're big ones too and so
I'll need some deadly poison that
Will lay them good and low.'

The man replied, 'This stuff right here
Is quite the best I've got.
'Twill kill a body in a tick
And it won't take a lot.

'So dealing with a few small rats
Will be a piece of cake,
Just half a gulp will kill them all
In less than half a shake.'

The young man grabbed the poison,
He gave the man a crown,
And then he bought some food and wine
Before he left the town.

He put the poison in the wine
And thought of his new wealth.
He thought, 'Now with this wine, my friends
Can both drink to my health.'

It made him laugh to think of them.
'Cheers', in his mind he said.
And then he pictured both of them
Flat on the ground stone dead.

Well there it is, why drag it out,
For everything progressed
In just the way that I am sure
That you've already guessed.

When he returned the other two –
Those evil, scheming men,
Attacked him with an awful force
And killed him there and then.

'Well, now it's done,' the first one said.
'I think I need a drink.'
A bottle was then opened up
In less than half a wink.

He took a mighty slug of wine,
His friend there did the same,
And in a tick we see the end
Of their black-hearted game.

For both collapsed upon the ground
And not a word was said,
They were completely out of it –
For both of them were dead.

They'd searched for Death and found him too
And he had laid them low,
'And now I say,' the Pardoner said
'There's one last thing to know,

'And that is when the old man warned
Death lingered by the tree,
He spoke the truth as I am sure
That you can clearly see.

'And so good friends, please be content
If you have all you need,
And do not stoop to evil ways
To satisfy your greed.

'Just be content with what you've got
And you'll be happy then,
So praise the Lord, my tale is told
And so I say – Amen!'

And so the Host and Pardoner
Embraced as well they might

EPILOGUE TO THE PARDONER'S TALE

Well once the Pardoner was done
A silence reigned supreme,
For everyone was overcome
By old Death's evil scheme.

But finally the Pardoner spoke
For from but one small glance
He'd seen an opportunity –
He had espied a chance

To sell some pardons for he saw
He'd got beneath their skins
And every one was thinking of
His own dire, tawdry sins.

'Step up my friends,' says he, 'for I
Have here within my store
Ancient relics from the Pope
And pardons by the score.

'And all I want is but a coin,
A shilling will suffice.
You'll be absolved of all your sins –
It's cheap at half the price.

'You all should thank your lucky stars
That I can – in a flash,
Forgive your sins – and it will cost
A paltry sum of cash.

'So who's the first to step this way
For you all have the need
To seek a pardon for your lust,
Your malice, hate and greed.

'For surely no-one here can claim
To truly be angelic,
So who will show the way and kiss
My ancient, holy relic?'

Then turning to the Host he cried,
'Step up and be the first
For out of everybody here
Your sins must be the worst.'

Well our good Host then raised his hand
And looking very vexed,
He said, 'No chance – you'll ask if I
Will kiss your backside next.'

The Pardoner fell silent then,
His face turned brightest red,
For he was angry and distraught
By what the Host had said.

He thought it disrespectful
To someone of his worth.
He really couldn't bring himself
To share the good Host's mirth.

As for the Host, he clearly saw
He'd gone a step too far,
He was concerned his comments now
This lovely day would mar.

But then the worthy Knight stepped in
And said, 'No more of this.
Dear Host please give the Pardoner
A kind embrace or kiss.'

And so the Host and Pardoner
Embraced as well they might.
This brought a smile of pleasure to
The good, peace-making Knight.

'So all is well,' the Host declared,
His confidence now growing.
'Let's carry on our way and keep
Our happy game a-going.'

'I have been busy marrying
For I've been wed five times.'

THE WIFE OF BATH'S PROLOGUE

The Wife of Bath was eager now
To have a little go.
She said, 'Before I start, there's this
I want you all to know.

'In life we learn as we go on.
Experience is the thing,
And from it we discern so much,
For knowledge it doth bring.

'And one thing I have surely learnt
From my most busy life
Is that the state of marriage brings
Much misery and strife.

'For while our good friend Chaucer spent
His life just spinning rhymes,
I have been busy marrying
For I've been wed five times.

'And of this chequered, motley bunch
Whatever can I say?
I guess that each could claim to be
Half decent in his way.

'Now is it wrong to do as I –
Should I have just refrained
From being wed more than the once –
Should I have just abstained?

'But then I think the Lord has said
That all of us must try
To do our bit and to go forth
And try to multiply.

'And anyway, good Abraham
And worthy Jacob too
Had many wives and both this pair
Were holy through and through.

'Virginity is fine indeed –
Young maids are free to shun
The marriage bed – it doesn't suit
The likes of everyone.

'For as you know, in life my friends
All speak with different voice,
And everyone is free to make
Their individual choice.'

The Pardoner reflected then,
'I thought to take a wife.'
She said, 'Best think awhile before
You thus commit for life.

'Now as I've said, I have been wed
Five times and I have had
Three husbands who were good as gold
And two who were quite bad.

'The good ones were both rich and old.
I treated them like kings,
And in return they bought for me
All kinds of pretty things.

'The bad ones, well, in time I tamed
Their selfish, wilful ways
But on the road I had some tough
And most unhappy days.

'But now I'm free again to wed
As they're all in the grave.
And you may ask me, do I now
Another husband crave?

'And I would answer truthfully –
Marry again? Why not?
Yes I would gladly take a man
And tie another knot.

'But of my husbands let me now
Stop speaking – I will cease
Prattling on about them all,
I'll let them rest in peace.

'I'll leave their souls safe there to share
Our precious Lord's great glory,
And if you will all bear with me
I'd like to tell my story.'

'For we old women know a lot,
Oh yes, indeed we do.'

THE WIFE OF BATH'S TALE

This tale of mine is set way back
When Arthur ruled our land,
A king of so much grace and charm –
So valiant and grand.

And then it came to pass one day
A knight of lusty turn
Espied a maiden by a stream
And how his lust did burn.

He followed her and then he took
Her maidenhead by force,
And then without a backward glance
He got back on his horse.

The news of this horrendous act
Soon spread and it did stoke
The ire and bitter anger of
All decent-minded folk.

They sent a message to the king
That was both loud and clear.
'We will not tolerate this stuff –
We'll have no raping here.'

Good King Arthur saw at once
From what his people said
There was but one thing to be done –
The knight must lose his head.

But the ladies of the court
And Arthur's sweet queen too,
Most strangely pleaded for the knight,
They took a different view.

They thought to execute the knight
Was really just too much.
They advocated earnestly
A somewhat softer touch.

And so the King said to the Queen,
'I leave his fate to you.'
And when the bad knight heard of this
He sighed and whistled 'Phew!'

The Queen then told the knight to come
Into her presence there,
She said, 'Don't think your life's now safe
For you still need beware.

'But I will spare you if you can
Tell me the answer to
The question I propose to ask –
The test I have for you.

'So tell me knight – what is it that
All women most desire?
And if you get it right I will
Release you from this mire.

'What is it that they want the most –
Do you know the answer?
If you've a mind – then take a guess,
I know you are a chancer.

'So Sir, your fate lies in my hands,
Don't think you can relax,
For if you get this question wrong
Your neck will feel the axe.

'But if the risk appears too great
To answer speedily,
Then you can take a year to think
And then come back to me.

'Just give your sworn and solemn oath
That you'll return next year.'
The knight replied he would, but hid
A sly, conceited sneer.

He thought, ''Twill be a piece of cake –
For every lass I see,
Why I will ask her what she wants
And she'll reveal to me

'The simple answer to this quest
The Queen has set me here,
And I'll be back to save my head
This time next year, no fear.'

Well, life is never quite like that
For every girl he met
Had her own view on what it was
A woman wants to get.

Some said a woman yearned the most
For jewels and such like treasure,
While others vowed that women craved
The most for sensual pleasure.

Some said all women liked to laugh,
Have fun above all things,
And hob-nob with nobility
And stroll around with kings.

And others that he asked were sure
That women liked to be
Flattered and adored and loved –
To worship them was key.

They said the thing that made their hearts
Flutter fit to burst
Was when a man paid court to them,
Oh yes, this came out first.

And so the knight rode on but now
He was quite dejected,
For others told him what they wished
Was just to be respected.

They wanted men to treat them well
And worship at their feet
Because they found them lady-like,
Soft-spoken and discreet.

The more all these conflicting views
Befuddled his poor head,
The more that he became convinced
He was as good as dead,

For there was but one answer that
Would satisfy the Queen,
And if he got the answer wrong
He knew what it would mean.

But which, if any, of these girls
Was on the proper track,
Could any of them get the Queen
From off his weary back?

'Twas as he pondered this one day
In sombre, downcast mood,
That in a leafy wood, a sight
Quite lovely did intrude.

Four and twenty girls so fair
Were dancing in a glade,
He watched them with enraptured eyes
While hidden in the shade.

Then softly he approached them
To see if he could learn
The answer to the question that
Within his soul did burn.

But just as he drew near the girls
All vanished into air
And left an old, foul-looking hag
Just crouching lamely there.

She was as ugly as could be,
Her every awful feature
Combined to make what surely was
A quite horrendous creature.

Enquiringly she looked at him.
The knight aghast, pulled back,
But in a crackling voice she spoke
And said, 'Good knight, alack,

'Tell this poor wretch just what you seek
For searching I am sure
Is what you do, but ask me sir
And you will search no more,

'For we old women know a lot,
Oh yes, indeed we do,
We may be old and wrinkled but
We know a thing or two.'

The knight replied with gusto then,
His every hope a-fire,
'Good mother, I have need to know
What ladies most desire.

'If I can't solve this problem,'
The knight then bowed his head,
Then looking up with soulful eyes,
He said, 'I'm good as dead.'

The ancient crone then spoke and thus,
'It is your lucky day,
For I can help you, but there is
A price you'll have to pay.

'So first of all, give me your hand
And swear you will be true,
That if I give you help, you will
Do all I ask of you.'

'Upon my life and honour too,
Old lady, I agree.'
The knight was overjoyed and said,
'Your words could set me free.'

'Your life will now be safe,' she croaked
'You can depend on me.
I'll save you from the axe, and this
Brave knight, I guarantee.'

And then she whispered in his ear,
Her wisdom she did share,
And then they made their way to court,
The knight now free of care.

And so it came to pass, the knight
Most confident and keen
To give his answer – stood before
The court and England's Queen.

For he was now quite certain that
He knew just what to say.
He bowed low to the Queen and said,
'I'm here to keep my day.

'I have returned to face my fate
Of freedom or the tomb.'
The Queen commanded silence then –
It fell upon the room.

And then the bold knight's voice rang out.
Would his fine words backfire?
Did he really know for sure
What women all desire?

'My Queen, I humbly now divulge
What women most require.
What they all want most fervently –
What all of them desire.

'They wish to have the same degree
Of honour and respect
That their good husbands, from their wives
Quite rightfully expect.

'The husbands must not put themselves
Above their wives – for then
They are the masters, and shrewd girls
Do not want this from men.

'They wish to be their equals,
And is this so amiss?
The ladies fair are all agreed,
They want no more than this.'

Well, what a gasp went up right then
From round the court-room there.
As for the knight, I must here tell
He said a silent prayer

Of thanks for as he looked around
He saw that all agreed,
He'd spoken well and truthfully –
His life was spared indeed.

The gracious Queen then bowed her head
To show her pleased assent,
And all around the court there was
Not one word of dissent.

'He's saved himself,' a lady cried,
And all then cried as one,
And then the old crone came to him,
She said, 'Well spoken son.'

But then she asked for all to heed –
It was the strangest scene
For the unsightly croaking crone
Addressed the gracious Queen.

''Twas I who told the truth of it,
What women want – and he
Said in return that he would do
Quite anything for me.

'Whatever boon I asked of him
He would with pleasure do.
This was our deal and now sweet Queen,
This deal, I hold him to.

'And so I say to you, Sir Knight
As I have saved your life,
I ask that you now grant this wish –
You take me for your wife.'

Well that caused quite a stir in court.
The poor knight, he turned white.
I think it's true, that in his life
He'd never felt such fright.

He cried, 'I know this was our deal,
But please, for heavens sake,
Think again – ask anything,
But give this knight a break.

'Take all my money – everything,
But madam, leave me free,
A match between the two of us
Was never meant to be.'

The horror on his face was plain
For all at court to see.
The crone replied, 'You promised that
You'd grant my wish to me.

'And I will be your wife and yes
You'll love me way above
All other women in the world –
I'll be your only love.'

'My only love!' the knight cried out.
His face turned deep, dark red,
But even so he had no choice
For he was forced to wed.

The Queen insisted that he paid
The debt he owed the crone,
So there was nothing he could do,
Except of course to groan.

The Queen gave him the starkest choice,
The toughest, direst warning.
'You'll face the axe if you don't wed
This lady in the morning.'

The knight was cornered, this he knew,
He owed the crone his life,
And like the fact or like it not
He'd got himself a wife.

So they were married and of course
Once the vows were said,
The knight as was the normal thing
Must take his wife to bed.

And so they lay abed, beside
The other lying there.
The knight was so resentful and
Thought life was just unfair.

He tossed and turned and did his best
To keep himself well clear
Of going near his wife – she said,
'Is something wrong my dear?

'Is this the way a bold, young knight
Deals with his brand new bride?
For I can see my presence here
You really can't abide.

'And yet I am your spouse and yes
Your most devoted wife.
And don't forget that it was I
Who saved your wayward life.'

He said, 'It's not my fault, it's that
You're ugly, old and plain.
To act as though you love someone
Is very hard to feign.'

'Is that the problem?' she replied.
'Well, I can put that right.'
He thought, 'The only remedy
Is if I lose my sight!

'For then I couldn't see this hag,
This apparition here.'
She looked at him and said, 'Don't fret,
I'll put it right, my dear.'

'Things cannot be put right,' he cried.
'It's all too late – for you
Just cannot change the way you look
Whatever you may do.

'You're old and crinkly – ugly too,
Abominable and dire.
You're quite repellent to a man –
You're what men don't desire.'

She smiled at him and from her mouth
One yellow tooth did sprout.
'At least there is one thing you can
Be unconcerned about,

'You'll never be a cuckold for
I'll never be two-faced
For my foul ways and ugliness
Will surely keep me chaste.

'For they are guardians – there's no doubt,
And they'll keep me demure,
You'll always have a faithful wife
Who's virtuous and pure.

'But now dear husband, hear me well,'
She said in rasping voice,
'I'll help you sort this whole thing out
But you must make a choice.

'You can choose to have me stay
Just as I am right now,
Old and ugly – bowed and bent,
White haired with wrinkled brow,

'But still a good and loving wife
Who's dutiful and true,
A wife who'd never cheat or be
Unfaithful unto you.

'Or would you rather I became
A young girl, fun and witty,
So full of life – a gorgeous sight,
Lithesome, sleek and pretty.

'If this is what I thus became
Great jealousy would gnaw
Throughout your being, for you'd think
That every man I saw

'Would fall for me – and you would think
They'd had their way with me,
And your whole life would soon become
Engulfed in misery.'

The puzzled knight, he scratched his head.
What choice should he now make?
What kind of wife would be the best?
He cried, 'For heavens sake.'

So in the end he just gave up,
He raised his hands on high,
He looked down on his ugly wife
And then said with a sigh,

'My dearest wife, my lady love,
I don't know what to do
And so I think it best by far
To leave it up to you.

'Use your great wisdom to decide –
Whatever you think best
This knight will find agreeable
And think himself well blessed.'

'So I can play the master here?'
The old hag asked the knight.
'You surely can,' he then replied,
'And do what you think right.'

'Well kiss me then,' the hag replied,
'And may I lose my life
If I don't prove to be for you
A fair and faithful wife.'

She disappeared behind a screen
So that he couldn't see,
And then she called out lovingly,
'Dear husband, come to me.'

And when the knight went to his wife
With massive trepidation
He found the most amazing thing –
There'd been a transformation.

For now she was a lovely girl,
Red lips and flowing hair,
An hourglass figure, long sleek legs,
A sight both sweet and fair.

She fell into his outstretched arms.
He thought, 'This is pure bliss.'
He held her tight and they exchanged
A passionate, long kiss.

And thus it was by treating her
With honour and respect
He'd got much more than any knight
Should reasonably expect.

By giving her what *she* desired
He had obtained a wife
Who was quite beautiful and who
Would love him all his life.

The Wife of Bath cried out, 'That's it!
The end of this my tale.
And as its moral clearly shows
A good wife can prevail.

'And so I say, for heavens sake
Send us good men in bed,
But let us get the upper hand
Sweet Jesus, once we're wed!'

'Let him speak,' the Summoner
Said with a nasty sneer

THE FRIAR'S PROLOGUE

When the Wife of Bath was done
The Friar up and cried,
'Bless you my dear and what a tale,
And goodness – what a bride!

'You raise important issues in
The story you have told,
But may I make a comment here,
If I may be so bold,

'And say that here is not the place
To thus disseminate
These weighty matters – there's no time
To start up a debate.

'We'll leave all this to others now,
For I'd say – if you please,
This is for schools of learning and
For universities.

'Let them discuss the pros and cons
Of all you've raised today,
For now is not the time for us
To ruminate this way.

'Our tales should be for merriment,
We're here to have some fun,
Philosophy and all such things,
I think we ought to shun.

'And now,' the Friar slyly said
As he glanced furtively,
Towards the Summoner who stood
Propped up against a tree.

'I'd like to tell a story too
And it is all about
A Summoner – a worthless chap,
A proper pain – a lout.

'Now I mean no offence, but friends
You surely must admit
That Summoners are folk who lack
All kindliness and wit.

'They hand out summonses to all
Who fornicate and such.
God help you if a Summoner
Should get you in his clutch.'

'Now hang about,' our Host cried out,
'We'll have politeness here.'
'Let him speak,' the Summoner
Said with a nasty sneer.

'He can say what e'er he likes
But when it is my turn,
Well then I'll get revenge, for I
Will cause *his* ears to burn.

'For he's a Limiter – and I
Will show just what I think
Of people just like him who beg
For what they eat and drink.'

'For mercy's sake – let's have some peace,'
Our Host cried, spreading balm
Upon the quarrel – once again
He tried to keep things calm.

Whatever would we all have done
Without that good man there,
Doing everything he could
To keep things nice and fair.

'Pray silence,' he declared, 'for by
Our own dear, sweet Messiah,
I'll hear this tale and so will you,
So speak up now, good Friar.'

He took him off to where they take
All evil, selfish men

THE FRIAR'S TALE

Close to where I live there dwelt
A pompous, proud archdeacon
Who liked to think his every act
Was like a pious beacon

For poor, lost sinners everywhere,
He really thought that he
Had the right to thus impose
Just any old decree.

And he would make quite sure that all
His flock were duty bound
To live within the law, but if
This harsh man ever found

That anyone was guilty of
The sin of fornication,
Adultery or drunkenness
Or evil fabrication,

Or thievery of any kind
Especially from a church,
My goodness, in a tick he'd knock
That person off their perch.

He wouldn't stand for it you see,
Or any such shortfall,
But I must say he hated those
Foul lechers most of all.

And anyone he caught he made
Pay out a whacking fine,
He showed no mercy – always took
The very hardest line.

In his employ he had a man –
A Summoner by trade,
The meanest piece of awful work
The good Lord ever made.

He had a clutch of spies that he
Would use to tell him where
A lecher lived and then he'd draw
The lecher to his snare.

And once he'd got him he would say,
'I'll let you off this time,
But you must tell of others who
Are guilty of this crime.'

*(And then the Friar paused and said
That he'd hold nothing back.
He said, 'I'm not afraid of our
Crass Summoner's attack.*

'For he has no authority
And no jurisdiction
Over Friars – so I'll assert,
Though it may cause some friction,

'Just what I like – for Summoners
Deserve what people say,
For everybody thinks they are
A pest in every way.'

The Summoner called harshly then –
Annoyed but in control,
With flashing eyes he shouted out,
'The devil take your soul.'

'Shut up – pipe down – give it a rest,'
It was our Host again.
'This bickering between you two
Has now become a pain.

'Get on with your story Friar,
Just tell it your own way.
The Summoner must live with it –
Don't spare the rod I say.'

The Friar said that anyone
Had right to thus complain
But it would not deter him – so
He set off once again.)

And so this Summoner would use
His power to impose
A summons with a heavy hand
On anyone he chose.

And often the archdeacon
Was kept right in the dark
Concerning all the goings on
Of this malignant shark.

That Summoner, that tyrant had
Loose wenches in his pay,
And this is what he chose to do –
He used them in this way.

He would encourage them to go
And sleep with good Lord Jack,
Or Reverend Robert or Sir Hugh –
Then when the wench came back,

He'd get her to recount the sin
Of each poor, set-up chap,
And then he'd smile for he would see
Who'd fallen for his trap.

He'd send a writ but tell each fool
Pay up and I'll delete
All record of your sin – be sure
I will then be discreet.

Of course they always sent the cash
When he applied the screw,
And so he always got his way
And thus his profits grew.

He'd use all forms of blackmail and
Skulduggery to con
The unsuspecting fools and then
His pious face he'd don,

And then pretend he sympathised
With their predicament,
And that in their debauchery
No harm was ever meant.

So all in all, a nasty bloke,
The worst to meet by far,
But Summoners are all like this,
That's just the way they are.

So now my friends, let's to my tale
And find this chap one day –
It is to see a widow that
This scoundrel makes his way.

He hopes to get her to fork out
A sum that is quite large,
To settle an account that is
A quite fictitious charge.

But as he makes his way to see
This destitute old dear,
He meets a striking yeoman who
Accosts him with great cheer.

The yeoman said, 'Good sir, pray tell
Where do you go today?
You seem to be a man possessed
As you rush on your way.'

The Summoner – he paused awhile
And then he said, 'Fine sir,
I'm off to see a widow
With whom I would confer.

'She owes some rent that is now due
Unto my lord and thus
She is required to pay at once
Or he'll create a fuss.'

'Well bless my soul,' the yeoman cried.
'You are a bailiff then.
Well I'm one too and are we not
The very best of men.'

And so they bonded instantly
For all birds of a feather
Will feel a sympathy and they
Will always stick together.

And thus in but a moment
They spoke to one another
As if they'd found a long-lost friend –
As if they'd found a brother.

Now take good heed, the Summoner
Did not tell of the fact
Of what he was – he wished to keep
His image quite intact.

For as we've said, all Summoners
Are base and very low,
They are the sort of fellows that
Nobody wants to know.

And then this chap, the Summoner,
That evil piece of work,
Said with a furrowed brow and with
A most unpleasant smirk,

'So tell me everything, good sir,
Of how you con the hicks,
Just tell your every little ruse
And all your subtle tricks.'

The yeoman answered with a sigh,
'My master keeps me short
So if I didn't use my wits –
Well then I'd toil for naught.

'So I use every rotten trick
And violence sometimes too,
Just anything to get my ends –
Yes, any ruse will do'

The Summoner, he clapped his hands,
He said, 'If truth I tell –
I will admit to you alone –
I do all that as well.

'I really could not live if I
Did not resort unto
Extortion – it's the only way
A bailiff can get through.

'Well what a pair we truly make,
We ply the self-same games,
By God, good sir, I think it's time
That we exchanged our names.'

The yeoman paused and then a smile
Appeared upon his face.
'I come from somewhere that you know,
A strange and awful place.

'It is a place you've often heard
Of many others tell,
For, my friend, I am a fiend –
My dwelling place is hell!

'And just like you I have a cause
That I pursue today,
I journey through the world to look
For unsuspecting prey.'

The Summoner cried, 'Lord above!
You say you've come from hell,
And yet you look just like a man –
You fooled me and right well.'

The devil said, 'You surely know
We fiends can change at will,
We can become an ape or man,
A Harry, Tom or Bill.

'Even an angel if we wish,
It doesn't take much skill,
For we can change to anything
And do it all at will.'

The Summoner then asked, 'Why choose
To travel in disguise?
Why not just show your proper self
Or would this be unwise?'

'There are reasons to be sure,'
The devil then replied,
'Why it is best to cover up
Who really lurks inside.

'I could explain – and yet, dear sir,
You wouldn't understand,
So just accept there are sound grounds
Why we are underhand.

'But this I tell you my dear friend,
If you now stick with me,
You'll learn a lot of evil and
A better rogue you'll be.

'You'll know enough of devil's work
To set yourself to be
A lecturer in all our works
At university.

'But now perhaps you would prefer
I leave you here alone,
Perhaps you would be happier
To travel on your own.'

'What!' the Summoner cried out.
'Leave you to travel on,
When I can learn of more sly ways
In which to work a con.

'Oh no, dear friend or devil – sir,
Whatever be your name,
I beg you now to teach me please
Your every dodgy game.

'For we have sworn to be true friends,
Each unto the other,
Indeed, good sir, you do appear
To be just like a brother.'

So off they went both now intent
To spend that sunny day
In doing evil – looking for
Some soul on whom to prey.

They shortly came across a man
Who made his weary way
Sat atop a farm-yard cart
Quite laden down with hay.

Strong horses pulled the heavy cart,
They struggled in the mud
Caused by a sudden fall of rain
That almost caused a flood.

The carter urged his horses on.
'Come Scottie – Brock,' he cried.
The horses couldn't budge the cart
However hard they tried.

So then the carter changed his tone.
He yelled – his face turned red.
'The devil take the lot of you,'
Angrily he said.

To this the Summoner remarked
To the old devil there,
'He offered you the chance to take
His cart into your care.

'He gave the whole shebang to you,
The horses, cart and hay,
So why don't you just grab it all
And take the lot away.'

'Don't be fooled,' the devil said.
'I heard his every word,
But what you think he said is not
What this old man inferred.

'It was but an expression,
Don't take it literally,
Just wait a tick and quickly now
We'll see what we will see.'

And sure enough the carter whacked
His horses on their flanks.
And in a tick the cart broke free,
The carter yelled his thanks.

Now free of mud the cart moved off
And headed up the hill,
The carter urged his horses on
With kindly words and skill.

He cried out, 'Well done Scottie,
You really are a star,
And as for you dear Brock – for sure
You are the best by far.

'So take the strain and pull away,
And Grey Boy, you're the one
To have around when heavy work
Is needing to be done.'

The carter urged those horses on,
The cart moved at a crawl,
And when it picked up speed – he cried,
'The good Lord save you all!

'Bless you my lovely horses – you
Have served me well this day.'
And then the carter trundled off
Astride his pile of hay.

'So there it is,' the devil said.
'I'm sure you see, dear brother,
Though the carter said one thing,
He really meant another.'

And so they travelled on and then
The Summoner exclaimed,
'This is where the widow lives
Whom I have named and shamed.

'For she's been told she owes a sum,
Twelve pence it is and I
Intend to get it even though
It's all based on a lie.

'We'll go and see her now and yes
We'll have some fun and sport,
And if she doesn't pay the sum,
We'll haul her off to court.'

And so that evil Summoner
Banged on the widow's door.
He cried, 'You drunken sot, don't you
Go hiding on the floor.

'I bet you've got a friar in there,
Or priest somewhere inside,
Come out you lustful crone – there is
Nowhere that you can hide.

'I have a summons here for you
That at great pains I've brought,
And you must answer to all this
At the archdeacon's court.

'You're due there in the morning and
Be sure that you're not late.'
The poor old widow there inside
Was now in quite a state.

She threw the door wide open,
And cried, 'Oh mercy please.
Oh leave me be, I'm innocent,
I'm begging on my knees.

'I couldn't walk to court or ride,
I'm old and too infirm
As anybody in these parts
Will readily confirm.

'Can't you write the charges down
Whatever they may be,
And save me from this journey and
Then act in court for me.'

'That I can,' the Summoner
Most readily replied,
'But you must pay twelve pence right now,
Then I will turn the tide,

'And pretty well, I'll guarantee
I'll get you off this charge,
So cough up now – for truthfully
The sum is not that large.

'And be assured, I don't enjoy
This monetary extraction,
I feel your pain and get no gain
From making this transaction.'

The widow looked into his face,
Despicable and scary,
And then she cried out desperately,
'O blessed Virgin Mary!

'How in this wicked, tortured world,
Immeasurable and wide
Would an old woman ever have
Just hanging at her side

'Twelve shiny pence – a princely sum –
If you step through my door
You'll see how wretchedly I live,
That I am very poor.'

The Summoner looked fiercely then
With wrinkled, furrowed brow,
He said, 'It would be best for you
If you pay up right now.'

There was no sign of sympathy
As he stood harshly there.
She cried, 'I have done nothing wrong,
This really isn't fair.'

He said, 'If you don't find the cash,
I'll use my other plan
And start off commandeering now
Your greasy frying pan.

'I let you off once in the past.
You cheated on your spouse.
That poor, dear chap who really was
As harmless as a mouse.'

'That's a lie,' the widow cried.
'I loved my dear old man,
And as for you, I don't care if
You take my frying pan.

'Take everything I've got you fiend,
Yes and the pan as well,
And with your worthless evil hide
Just take the lot to hell.'

Oh how she ranted and she raved –
The devil standing by
Asked, 'Is this what you really want
Or is it just a lie?

'Now widow Mabel tell me please,
Was it the truth you spoke?
Or were you angry – was it just
A hot ill-tempered joke?'

'Upon my life,' old Mabel said,
Annoyed and undeterred,
'The devil take him and the pan,
I meant it – every word'

The Summoner was livid too.
He said, 'I'll take the lot,
All your clothes – your house-goods too,
Everything you've got.'

But then the devil intervened.
He said, 'Just let things be.
Why are you cross for now, my friend,
She's given you to me.

'For now you are my property,
The frying pan as well,
So you must come with me – tonight
You'll be with me in hell.'

And as he spoke, he swooped upon
The Summoner and then,
He took him off to where they take
All evil, selfish men.

For there's a special place in hell
Where they recognise
These Summoners – to pay them back
For all their nasty lies.

And that is where our evil friend
Found himself that day,
And where he saw there surely was
An awful price to pay.

And so I say to Summoners
And to our good friend here,
Be well aware there is a lot
That you should rightly fear.

I would advise you change your ways,
If not – there is no doubt,
You'll pay – for that old devil there
Will surely seek you out!

They swarmed around like honey bees

THE SUMMONER'S PROLOGUE

Well it will come as no surprise
The Summoner with us
Was pretty mad about this tale –
Oh, how he made a fuss!

He stood up in his stirrups,
He shook from head to toe.
'Don't listen to this stupid Friar,
Whatever does he know?

'He says he knows of hell – he tries
To come out looking smart,
Of course we know that friars and fiends
Are never far apart.

'That's why he's able here to speak
Of devils and of hell,
To him it's all familiar,
He knows them very well.

'These friars are such a useless bunch
With egos far too big,
Full of their own importance but
They are not worth a fig.

'So is it any wonder
That Summoners despise
Fat friars, for they always tell
The most atrocious lies.

'But let me briefly tell you of
A Friar who had a dream,
Forgive me if I speak of hell,
I don't mean to blaspheme,

'But it was hell this Friar saw –
He walked there in the fire,
But found no trace of men like him –
He saw no other Friar.

'Though guided by an angel
Who knew his way around,
The Friar was overcome with fear
At everything he found.

'And when he saw no brothers there
In that awful place,
He said, 'There are no friars here
Suffering disgrace.

'So are there none in hell – are they
In heaven with the Lord?'
'The angel smiled, 'There's many here –
In fact there's quite a horde.'

'The Friar then asked, 'So are they in
A very special place?
Being friars I'm sure they're in
A higher state of grace.'

'The angel beckoned that vain man
And said, 'You are not wrong.
There is a place that some would say
They rightfully belong.'

'He took the Friar to Satan and
Said, 'May I, sir, prevail
Upon you now and ask if you
Will kindly raise your tail.'

'Satan did as he was asked
And from his backside then
Came tumbling a massive swarm
Of most disgruntled men.

'And when the Friar looked he saw
They were all friars too,
They had a special place all right,
And one that had no view.

'They swarmed around like honey bees,
Then acting all as one,
Their short excursion over now,
Their swarming now all done,

'They disappeared from whence they'd come –
When safely out of sight,
Old Satan dropped his tail and turned
Their day back into night.'

The Summoner then smiled a smile
To show his great disdain.
He said, 'I think from what I've told
I've made it very plain

'Just what I think of holy friars
From this my little taster,
Now to my tale – I'll not be called
A bothersome time-waster.

'But first one word to everyone,
Fat, thin or short or tall,
Excluding just that stupid Friar –
Kind wishes to you all.'

'You filthy dog – you'll pay for your
Unruly, foul backside.'

THE SUMMONER'S TALE

In Yorkshire dwelt a Friar who was
A Limiter as well,
And so as I've already said
Deserved a place in hell.

A Limiter – well he's a type,
Holds out his hand and begs.
This kind of friar, I am convinced
Is just one of life's dregs.

The Friar of whom I speak would preach
Anywhere he could,
And he'd proclaim to everyone
They should be chaste and good.

And then of course once he had got
The crowd tuned to perfection,
All fired up – in giving mood,
He'd take a quick collection.

And once he'd got the money in,
He'd close the sermon then
With '*Qui cum Patre*' and a bow
He'd set off once again.

And he would travel merrily,
He'd go from town to town,
And anyone who gave him cash,
He'd write their name right down,

Upon a tablet that he had,
The folk would watch him write.
He'd say, 'Because you gave to me,
I'll pray for you tonight.'

But once he left them – well this cur
Who seemed to be devout,
Would wipe the tablet clean at once,
He'd wipe their name right out.

So all his preaching was a sham,
Merely hocus pocus,
For conning cash from innocents
Was his only focus.

(But then the Friar in our midst
Let out a raucous yell,
'That's just a pack of rotten lies –
A monstrous tale you tell.'

'Oh do shut up,' our Host then cried.
'For love of Christ I say
Let the Summoner tell his tale,
Good Friar – please give way.'

And then he added pleasantly,
'Honest friend – dear Friar,
It's just a tale – it matters not
If he thus plays a liar.

'So please continue with your tale,
And Friar, don't you pout,
It's his turn now – so Summoner
I pray, leave nothing out.'

The Summoner picked up his tale,
Although it must be said
He looked annoyed – he flashed his eyes,
His face was flushed bright red.)

The Friar went from door to door
Taking cash at each,
And in return, such pious words
To these poor folk he'd preach.

Then finally he knocked upon
The door of one he knew,
A woman opened it – he said,
'Pray madam, how are you?'

She said that she was doing fine,
Her husband though was not,
She wrung her hands and cried aloud,
'I don't know what he's got.'

371

And so the Friar went within
And there tucked up in bed
Lay Thomas – a poor, sickly soul.
'Good-day,' the Friar said.

'So how are you today, old friend?
I've thought of you so often.'
As he spoke that wily Friar
Made a point to soften

The way he spoke – he tried to sound
Pious and concerned,
And only by close scrutiny
Could it have been discerned,

That all his talk was frippery,
For he cared not a jot
Whether Thomas got well soon
Or whether he did not.

As for Thomas, he lay there
Looking pale and weak,
'I need God's grace to make me well,
It's his kind help I seek.'

Of course the Friar saw his chance.
He said, 'Though I've not been
To see you for a while – I have
Been with you, though not seen.

'I've offered up so many prayers,
All said to make you well,
And they have cost me quite a lot
If truth I am to tell.

'For every time I said a prayer
I placed some money in
The coffers of the church to help
To wash away your sin.

'For if you then become quite free
Of sin – embrace the Lord,
Your sickness will be cured.' – thus spoke
That double-dealing fraud.

Poor Thomas lay there on the bed,
He'd heard all this before,
However much he gave the Friar,
He always wanted more.

He knew that sneaky, dodgy Friar
Was out to make him pay,
To find a way to gain more cash –
That's why he'd come today.

He'd taken so much in the past
And here he was again,
Old Thomas grimaced there and it
Was not caused out of pain,

At least not physical – it was
The thought of what would come,
For how much would the Friar want –
What would be this day's sum?

'O Thomas, Thomas, my dear son,'
The Friar slowly said,
'We've prayed for you both night and day
To raise you from this bed.

'At our church we've asked the Lord
To make you sound of limb,
Every day we're on our knees
Saying prayers to Him.

'And I am now convinced that you
Will very soon be well.'
Old Thomas thought then to himself,
'Friar – go to hell!'

He didn't voice his thoughts but said,
'However much you pray
And ask the Lord to make me fit,
However much I pay,

'It makes no difference – here I lie,
My sickness with me still,
I have to say I have my doubts
About your praying skill,

'For o'er the years I've paid to friars
A fortune and it's made
No difference – so I do not think
You're much good at your trade.

'In fact I have to say I don't
Have much time for friars,
They promise much but I have found
They're just a bunch of liars.

'And now my gold is nearly gone,
I'm almost broke and so
Don't give me more crass platitudes
For I don't want to know.'

The Friar of course had heard such talk
Countless times before
But he had many crafty wiles
Locked up within his store.

Yes – he knew how to gather cash
For he knew every trick.
He said, 'You do not give enough
That's why you are still sick.

'I know you've given in the past,
But Thomas, not that much.'
My that old Friar could tell a tale,
He had a sneaky touch.

But Thomas as he lay abed
Saw through his little game,
A thousand times he'd heard the Friar –
It always was the same.

'Give me some money, Thomas dear,
And I will pray for you,
And very soon the Lord will make
You feel as good as new.'

Oh yes, he'd heard this tripe before
But now he felt inclined
To tell the Friar to sling his hook –
That's what went through his mind.

But something else occurred to him,
He said, 'To ease my pain
I'll give to you and generously,
I'll gladly give again,

'But if I do, I ask that you
Should grant me one small boon;
If you agree you'll have my gift
Within your hand – and soon.'

The Friar readily agreed
And so old Thomas said,
'That which I give, you must now swear
You evenly will spread

'Amongst your fellow friars – for each
Must have an equal share,
I count on you to dole it out
So it's entirely fair.'

The Friar exclaimed, 'Rely on me,
And Thomas – have no doubt
Each friar will be quite satisfied
With how I deal it out.'

Thomas smiled and said, 'Well slide
Your hand right down the bed,
All the way until you feel
My gift – as I just said,

'A thing that I have hidden there,
Right beneath my bum,
And in its way I guess that it
Amounts to quite a sum.'

The Friar's heart then leapt for joy.
'That sounds all right,' he thought.
It sounded like it surely was
The kind of prize he sought.

A bag of money it must be,
And so he poked his hand
Into the bed and down into
That dark and private land.

His hand slid down until he felt
Thomas's backside,
He thought, 'Oh what a lousy place,
A pile of cash to hide.'

He groped about and furiously,
But then old Thomas sinned,
For noisily and with a smile
The sick, old man broke wind.

I swear there never, ever was
A horse that drew a cart
That let out such a thunderous sound
As Thomas' great fart.

The Friar jumped back angrily.
'By God's bones,' he cried.
'You filthy dog – you'll pay for your
Unruly, foul backside.

'You did that act on purpose then.
You have insulted me.'
The only thing that Thomas felt
Was overwhelming glee.

But as the Friar displayed his wrath
Some servants rushed right in,
They were concerned for Thomas as
They'd heard the angry din.

They chased the Friar from the house
With great hostility,
The Friar had never ever moved
With such agility.

In all his life he'd never felt
Such humiliation.
He was quite overcome with rage
And a deep frustration.

He wanted now to find a place
Where he'd get sympathy,
To speak to someone who would feel
A deal of empathy.

And so he made his way towards
A manor house close by,
He thought, 'This place is better than
Foul Thomas' pig-sty.'

Oh how he fumed – his anger boiled
Like red-hot cooking fat,
In all his life he'd never been
Insulted quite like that.

When the Lord came to the door
He said, 'Why Friar John
What ails you friend – you look as if
You have been put upon.'

'Put upon!' the Friar yelled.
'You put it mildly, friend.
You'll hear a tale you won't believe
If you, good sir, attend.

'A lousy little guttersnipe
Insulted me today,
For he abused this pious Friar
In a filthy way.

'He has insulted me and yes
From this one can construe
An insult to my order and
Our Holy Church there too.'

'Whatever did he do to you?'
The Lord then asked the Friar.
'Did he accuse you of a wrong,
Call you a cheat or liar?'

'Even worse,' the Friar replied.
And then he did impart
The details of the dreadful act,
He told him of the fart.

The lady of the house was there
And so she listened too,
And when he'd done the Friar said,
'Dear madam – what's your view?'

She said, 'It's nothing very much.
And I would say in fact
That this is just a silly man
And just a silly act.

'Poor old Thomas there, I think,'
The lady blithely said,
'Has gone a trifle soft inside
His muddled, stupid head.'

'Well possibly,' the Friar exclaimed,
'And though he's weak of limb
And sickly too, I do avow
I'll have revenge on him.

'I'll blacken his foul name abroad
Every time I preach.
You'll be astounded just how far
My angry words will reach.'

Now while the Friar turned bright red
And as his anger grew,
The Lord just sat there quietly
And let the Friar stew.

And then he said, 'How in the world
Could Thomas think of that?
If there's an answer to this thing
Well then I'll eat my hat.

'How did he think of such a ruse?
What a devious mind.
And could we using science solve
This problem – ever find

'A suitable solution,
That would tell us how to part,
Right into equal quantities
A thing quite like a fart.

'It can't be done, for it is just
A rumble in the air,
It surely isn't possible
To give each friar a share.

'Yet even so – it makes you think,
But now it hurts my head,
And so good Friar, I would suggest
We have some food instead.

'And please now calm yourself and keep
Your mind relaxed and level,
And as for Thomas, let him go
To hell and to the devil!'

And so they all sat down to eat
Beside a roaring fire,
And they were served a hearty meal
By the Lord's young Squire.

He had heard them speak and said,
'My Lord, I beg don't frown,
But if you'll give me some fine cloth
With which to make a gown,

'I'll tell you how it could be done,
How you could share a fart.'
The Lord, the Lady and the Friar
Thought he was being smart.

But then the Lord sat up and said,
'Now how could anyone
Do this thing? – but if you tell
How it could thus be done

'You'll have a bolt of finest cloth,
So give us your solution.
How could you share its noise and then
Its smelly air pollution?'

The Squire replied, 'You wait until
The day is fine and fair,
When all is calm – and there is no
Disturbance in the air.

'Then bring a cartwheel to the hall.
One that has twelve spokes.'
(The Lord looked ruefully – he thought,
'Is this one of his jokes?')

'And then my Lord invite to come
Twelve friars to this place
From the order that our friend
The Friar does embrace.

'Then tell each friar to place his nose
At a spoke's far end.
I would suggest a special place
For the Friar here – our friend.

'For he should place his nose beneath
The hub of the cartwheel,
A place that recognises thus
His ardent faith and zeal.

'And once the friars are at their spokes,
Then bring the fellow in,
And tell him that he must set off
His smelly, thunderous din,

'Right above the other side
Of the cartwheel's hub
To where our friend the Friar stoops –
And now here is the rub,

'For I will stake my life upon
The fact – that awful smell,
When once it leaves foul Thomas there
Will evenly propel,

'And reach the noses of the friars
As it passes round,
At the self-same moment as
They also hear the sound.

'Thus each friar has equal share
But the Friar here with us,
To recognise his merit will
Receive a special plus,

'For his nose being at the hub
Will have the biggest share,
And as he is of special worth
I think this right and fair.'

The Lord and his good lady too
Thought this was all first-class,
It offered a quite sound result
But with a touch of farce.

They said their young Squire had the brain
Of someone of renown
And promised that he would receive
The cloth to make a gown.

The Friar sulked with moody face,
He saw that at a stroke
The Squire had found an answer and
Made him butt of a joke.

And then the general feeling was,
Old Thomas was a wit,
He wasn't mad or stupid – no,
Not even just a bit.

To think of such a silly ruse
He must be fairly smart,
For thinking up a stunt like that
Was something of an art.

The Summoner then smiled at us
Just like a Cheshire cat,
There was no doubt he felt quite pleased,
It seemed apparent that

He had enjoyed himself and though
He might say I'm a liar,
I really think he loved the chance
To stick it to our Friar.

And then the Summoner declared,
'On such a sunny morn,
Time passes quickly for we now
Have reached fair Sittingbourne.

'So let us talk no more of Friars
Or Thomas' emission,
But rather bow in reverence
And in devout submission.

'And gratefully give thanks and clasp
Our hands and kneel and pray
That we've come safely to this place –
That we're well on our way.'

'It is a tale that will amuse.'

THE CLERK'S PROLOGUE

Now once again a voice rang out –
One we'd often heard.
'Pray Mister Clerk,' our Host cried out,
'You haven't said a word.

'You ride along just like a maid
Who is but newly wed,
Who contemplates the night to come
Within the wedding bed.

'Or are you meditating there
On some weighty question
Of great importance – well my friend,
This is my suggestion.

'Stir your stumps and cheer yourself
For Solomon has said
There is a time for everything –
At least that's what I've read.

'And you agreed to tell a tale –
This was, good sir – the deal,
So tell a tale to stir our souls
But not to make us feel

'Depressed and guilty or borne down
By sinning in the past –
You surely know some stirring tales,
Your knowledge must be vast.

'So dig down deep and tell us one,
But good sir, when you do
I humbly and most earnestly
Request one thing of you,

'To please use language of a kind
That we will understand,
Don't use the highfalutin words
Used by your learned band.

'Just keep it simple – to the point
From start right to the end
And then we'll get the gist of it –
So thank you kindly, friend.'

The Clerk with shyness then replied.
He said, 'Good Host, by God,
I'll do as you request, for now
I'm governed by *your* rod.

'For on our way to Canterbury
One and all agreed
That you'd take charge and to your rule
Each one of us would cede.

'And so I'll tell a little tale
That was once told to me
In Padua – which is of course
Somewhere in Italy.

'It is a tale that will amuse
But humbly I would say
It also has a moral so
Without undue delay

'I will begin and all I ask
As this sad tale I tell
Is your respectful silence and
That you all listen well.'

And then with hand on sword

THE CLERK'S TALE

In Saluzzo, in Italy,
A grand Marquis once ruled.
In courtesy and chivalry
He had been fully schooled.

Respected by his people,
He loved to hawk and hunt,
But there was just one issue that
He never would confront.

For pleasure was the main pursuit
Of this young noble's life,
And so he'd never ever thought
Of looking for a wife.

His people there were most concerned,
For though they thought him wise
And good in everything – they asked,
'What happens if he dies?

'For we'll be left right in the lurch.
What will become of us?'
And so they went to him and said,
'My Lord, excuse this fuss,

'But we are sick with worry,
For each of us among
This deputation, realise
That though you are still young,

'The years fly by and then one day
When your life's course is run,
When you are old – well what of us
If you don't have a son?

'You need an heir, dear Lord, and then
We all would feel assured,
For with an heir your province would
Be safe and well insured.

'We do not want to cause offence
Or show you disrespect
But surely Lord you have to see
The dastardly effect

'No heir to follow plainly has –
For we are all a-feared
That if within your palace now
No young are ever reared,

'Well, we'll be left bereft and then
A stranger just might take
Your province and might prove to be
A tyrant, fake or snake.

'A double-dealing devil or
A selfish fiend or worse.
And so we ask deliver us
From this potential curse.

'For if you die and leave no heir
'Twill cause us all such strife,
Good sir, for mercy's sake we beg
Please find yourself a wife.'

One who was there and thought to be
Wiser than the rest,
Spoke up with intensity,
He did his very best

To convince the Marquis that
He should be getting wed,
He spoke with passion and with force
And this is what he said.

'My Lord you've always been so good,
Considerate and kind,
And so I'm sure you'd like to give
Your people peace of mind.

'And though you may be scared to wed
And always wish to be
Forever sowing your wild oats,
Unshackled and quite free,

'We your people do believe
It's wrong to be alone.
You should now find a wife and have
Some children of your own.

'In fact we are prepared to look,
To find your perfect bride;
Somebody with the attributes
To stand there at your side.'

The Marquis answered them and thus –
Now anxious to dispel
Their fear and anguish – so he said,
'I know you all mean well,

'And for this reason, be assured
I do not take offence,
For I can see most readily
That what you say makes sense.

'And though I love my liberty,
I will – to ease your strife
Consent to marriage and will now
Agree to take a wife.

'But with regard to helping me,
Although it was well meant,
I'll make the choice – and so to this
I surely won't consent.

'But yes, I will agree to wed –
And I'll fulfil this task
And find myself a wife – but one
Important thing I ask,

'You each must swear on oath that you'll
Accept the wife I choose,
For I must make it very clear
That if you then refuse

'To accept the girl I want,
Well then I'll never wed.'
Everybody there that day
Was thrilled by what he said.

They readily agreed his terms
And so he picked a day
And said, 'I'll marry on this date,
Come whatever may.'

The people all agreed as one
That they were truly blest.
The Marquis for his part declared,
'I'll honour this request,

'But be assured, it is for you
That I now seek a spouse,
Someone who'll be a credit to
Your Marquis and his house.'

And then he set his court a-buzz,
He ordered there and then
Arrangements for a wedding day –
And though he told them when

This great occasion would take place,
Nobody had a clue
Who the Marquis meant to wed
Or what he planned to do!

In a hamlet quite close by
There lived an old man who
Was always short of cash but still
Was honest through and through.

He was the poorest of the folk
Who lived their sorry lives
Within the hamlet – but you know
How nature then contrives

To give a blessing to the poor
And this was here the case,
Because he had a daughter who
Was sweet and fair of face.

And she was just so virtuous,
Her every waking act
Was carried out with kindliness,
With thoughtfulness and tact.

And she did everything she could
To care for her old Dad –
But there is one surprising thing
That I must quickly add,

For this sweet girl, Griselda there
Had caught the roving eye
Of the Marquis on those days
When he'd been riding by.

And it must truthfully be said
His thoughts weren't just of lust,
He'd seen her goodness and he'd thought
She was a girl you'd trust.

He'd seen how hard she worked each day
And cared for her old Dad,
And so he'd reasoned many times,
Though folk would think him mad,

'If ever I should take a wife,
Griselda's who I'll wed
For I would gladly share my life
With that sweet girl,' he'd said.

Meanwhile arrangements hurried on,
A wedding was prepared,
Quite sumptuous, at massive cost
For no expense was spared.

Everything was in its place,
A wedding dress was made,
And carefully and tenderly
The lovely dress was laid,

Across a couch, in readiness
For a bride to wear,
But though the dress was ready now
There was no sweet bride there.

For who would wear it – no-one knew,
The Marquis wouldn't say.
Then in a flash the date arrived.
It was the wedding day!

All was ready – church and priest,
A feast, the guests, the lot.
Everything was waiting but
A bride to be was not.

The Marquis then appeared before
The lords and ladies there,
They wondered if he'd now produce
A bride out of thin air.

And then the Marquis spoke out loud.
He bade them follow him.
The lords and ladies looked askance.
Was this some idle whim?

He led them to the hamlet where
Griselda had no notion
Of what it meant when she espied
Approaching, a commotion.

She was fetching water when
The Marquis stopped outside
Her little home – she never guessed
She was his chosen bride.

He called to her and she approached
This man of such renown.
Most gingerly and carefully
She laid her pitcher down.

'Where is your father?' he enquired.
'Right here,' the girl replied.
And in a tick Janicula,
Her Dad stood at her side.

The Marquis took the old man's hand.
'Janicula,' he said,
'You know I'm sure that it's today
That I have said I'll wed.

'And yet I do not have a bride,
And so I say to you
There is but one in all the world
That truthfully will do.

'And that dear person lives right here.
She's standing by your side.
It is Griselda, your sweet girl
I wish to be my bride.

'Will you agree, Janicula.'
(The old man dropped his jaw.)
'To be my father – let me be
Your own dear son-in-law?'

The shocked old man was speechless.
Such thoughts rushed through his head.
Finally he spoke, 'My Lord
If 'tis your wish,' he said,

'Then readily I do agree
For I am of a mind
To do your will – for you have been
A Lord both wise and kind.'

The Marquis faced Griselda then,
He said, 'Your father here
Has said that you can marry me,
But what say you, my dear?

'Will you become my loyal wife?
But ere you do agree
There are some questions I must ask
And you must answer me.

'First of all, will you consent
To marry me today?
It must be now, there cannot be
A moment of delay.

'For if you wish to think about
This offer that I make,
Then it is speedily withdrawn
For, madam, you must take

'My hand in marriage right away
Or sweet girl, not at all,
And if you do you must submit
To all that may befall.

'And do my will, do all I ask,
And never try to be
Anything but loyal – true,
A faithful wife to me.'

Griselda there was filled with awe,
Bedazzled – overcome.
The words the Marquis spoke to her
Almost struck her dumb.

But finally she grew composed.
She said, 'I am not fit.
But if it is your wish, my Lord,
Then gladly I'll submit.

'I'll be your wife and promise here
To always do your will,
And if it cost my very life
I would obey you still.'

The Marquis clapped his hands with glee
And happily he cried
To everybody gathered there,
'Griselda is my bride!'

And so upon that very day
They wed and she became
Wife to the Marquis and enjoyed
Respect and love and fame.

And her unselfish qualities
Were always at the fore,
And she became the perfect wife
And all the people swore

She was the kindest person for
She always understood
How to help the people and
To do all that was good.

They thought that she was heaven sent,
A gift from God above,
And so they gave unstintingly
Their deep, unerring love.

And then, oh joy of joys! – this wife
Gave birth to their first child.
The Marquis was quite overwhelmed,
The people all went wild.

But for the Marquis, one thing marred
This blissful, new event,
It was a little girl the fates
On this occasion sent.

The Marquis wished to have a son
So he could be his heir,
But still he loved the darling girl
That he saw lying there.

'I know I'll have another child,'
He then told everyone.
'And when I do, I am convinced
That it will be a son.'

Now while the girl was but a babe
There came about a change.
The Marquis' behaviour
Became extremely strange.

He felt he needed to find out
How faithful and how true
His wife Griselda really was –
And would she really do

Everything he asked of her –
Was he truly blest
With a wife who'd carry out
His every last request?

And so he said to her one day,
'Do you agree to do
Anything I should desire
Or ever ask of you?

'For this is what you did avow
When you became my wife.'
Griselda said, 'Do what you will
With me and with my life.

'For I am yours to freely use
And handle as you will.
Whatever you may ask of me,
I swear I'll love you still.'

How perverse to think to test
His wife in such a way
And when she loved and honoured him
Each and every day.

And so one night the Marquis sent
One of his men to see
His wife within her chamber and
This man was told that he

Should test Griselda in a way
Most horrible to tell,
But I must here relate the facts
Of sadly what befell.

He told Griselda, 'I've been asked
By our good, noble Lord
To take your baby far away.'
And then with hand on sword

He grabbed the baby roughly –
He snatched Griselda's daughter
In such a way as to imply
He took her to her slaughter.

But what of poor Griselda?
Whatever did she do?
Did she shout and scream for help,
Get worked up in a stew?

Did she rave and carry on
As any mother would?
Especially one like this sweet girl
So fine and kind and good.

Well no – she sat there meekly like
A helpless fawn or lamb.
Perhaps she thought the action of
The man was but a sham.

But this was not the case – she thought
Her child was dead for sure,
Judging by the fearsome look
The fellow's face now wore.

She didn't weep or even sigh,
She sat there frozen still,
Even though she was convinced
This awful man would kill

The darling babe she loved so much,
But then the poor girl spoke,
Her words came out in whispers as
She tried then to invoke

A trace of sympathy within
The harsh man standing there.
She asked if she could hold her babe,
Kiss her and stroke her hair.

The man agreed – she took the babe
And with a heavy sigh
She said, 'Farewell my lovely girl
For sadly you must die.'

It was a dreadful sight to see,
Almost too much to bear.
Griselda though was resolute,
Did not display her care.

She kept her desperate pain inside –
Her torment and her dread,
And outwardly she kept quite calm.
'Please take the child,' she said.

'But do one favour for me now
Unless it is forbidden
Bury her with every care
So that she is well hidden.

'This is all I ask of you,
It is my one appeal.
I wouldn't want a roaming beast
To take her as a meal.'

Then with a face just like a mask,
Quite expressionless,
She looked upon the child and then
Gave her one last caress.

Gently then, with tenderness
She handed him the child.
She didn't show just how she felt
Her motherhood defiled.

The henchman of the Marquis took
The helpless babe away.
He took her to his master – said,
'I've done your work today.

'Here is the girl,' and then he told
Of all that had occurred,
Just how Griselda had behaved
And said no angry word.

The Marquis nodded quietly,
It surely did appear
That for Griselda's constancy
He had no cause to fear.

He told the man to take the babe
To Bologna where
His sister was to raise the child
And keep her in her care.

And then he said, 'Don't breathe a word
To anyone of this.
And now be gone,' – and then he gave
The child a single kiss.

The Marquis now observed his wife
To see if he could see
The slightest sign of anger in
Her personality.

Would she have changed towards him or
Would she be in a state,
And would her feelings for him now
Have changed from love to hate.

Well – however hard he looked
He could discern no trace
Of anger or resentment on
Her calm, adoring face.

She acted in the self-same way
As she always had.
She gave no indication that
She thought his actions bad.

Her love was all-encompassing,
Passionate and true,
Obedient as in the past,
And always keen to do

Everything the Marquis asked –
She acted just the same
And never mentioned her sweet child
Or ever spoke her name.

Four years passed by speedily
And then – oh happy news,
Griselda was with child again –
This once more did infuse

The Marquis's great court with such
Excited expectation,
It was the topic in the town
Of every conversation.

And then a handsome boy was born
But when he was but two,
The Marquis had the thought again
That he would turn the screw.

He'd test his wife in just the way
He'd tested her before.
You'd think that of her loyalty
He now could be quite sure.

But no – he was of jealous turn
And so he said one day,
'I do intend to treat our son
In just the self-same way

'As our daughter – so my dear,
I ask you to prepare
To say farewell for soon he'll be
No longer in your care.

'And he'll be taken in the night
As was your daughter too,
I tell you so this doesn't come
As such a shock to you.

'It's better if you hear the news
In this way – by degrees.
I ask for understanding and
For your forbearance please.'

Griselda answered him and thus,
'If this is your desire
Then I obey it willingly,
And with all patience, sire.

'Even if my children both
Are killed – I'll not be grieved,
For they have only brought me pain
Since first they were conceived.

'You are my Lord and master, sire,
So all I have to say,
My one and only duty is
To honour and obey.

'Accepting all you wish of me
And never reason why,
And even if you wished my death,
My Lord, I'd gladly die.

'Your love means everything and if
You sentenced me to death
I still would bless and pray for you
With my last dying breath.'

The Marquis stood with sombre face,
Though he now felt inside
A happiness that filled his heart
And made him burst with pride.

Oh such a loyal, caring wife –
But still he gave the word
To do unto his son the same
As to his girl occurred.

His henchman seized the lovely boy –
Griselda as before
Begged that her child be laid to rest
Deep down to thus ensure

No roaming beast would make a meal
Of her beloved son.
The henchman as he took the boy
Agreed this would be done.

But of course he really took
Her precious son away
To Bologna – where 'twas planned
The little lad would stay.

The Marquis then observed his wife –
Again he saw no trace
Of hatred or resentment in
Griselda's lovely face.

She was as constant and as true
As she'd been in the past,
So you would think that testing her
Would terminate at last.

But as the years passed by he still
Dwelt on Griselda's worth.
Did she still love him just as much
As at their union's birth?

So once again he set a trial.
This was his biggest lie.
A subterfuge, to test his wife
To see if she'd comply.

But first he wrote a letter to
His sister's spouse and he
Instructed him, 'Please bring my kin
Most swiftly back to me.

'Tell no-one who these children are.'
And in his note he said,
'Tell everyone the girl with you
Is coming here to wed

'The Marquis of Saluzzo who
Has said most graciously
That he will marry her and so
A Lady she will be.'

His daughter was now fully grown.
A maiden of some beauty,
And she did all they asked of her,
She saw it as her duty.

She was attired in lovely clothes
And with her brother too
She headed for Saluzzo and
The wedding rendezvous.

Meanwhile again, the Marquis spoke
Unkindly to his wife.
Griselda listened and his words
Cut through her like a knife.

But still she was compliant – calm
As she then heard him say,
'Though you have been a loyal wife
You must leave here today.

'My people wish it – they have said
It is my obligation
To marry someone closer to
My rank and to my station.

'And I must tell you honestly,'
He said to her dismay,
'That as we speak, my wife to be
Now travels on her way,

'To join me and to marry me,
So now you know it all.'
Griselda was impassive as
She heard of her downfall.

She said, 'I always knew my Lord
Of my unworthiness
To be your wife – in honesty
I here and now profess

'That there is no comparison
Twixt you my Lord and me,
For I was born of lowly stock
And raised in poverty.

'So to my father I'll return
And there I'll live my life,
And there I'll pray most fervently
For you and your new wife.

'And all my gems and fine attire
I readily return,
But there is one small wish I make,
I hope you will not spurn.

'Let me retain the tattered smock
That I wore when we met,
In recompense for what I gave,
It will repay this debt.

'For I leave here my maidenhead –
I cannot take it hence,
So give me this, my tattered smock
By way of recompense.'

'For mercy's sake – retain the smock,'
The Marquis cried bereft.
He found he pitied her but still
He turned around and left.

So poor Griselda took each shred
Of fine cloth from her back,
And pulled the worn out, tattered smock
That looked just like a sack

O'er her head – and then she left,
The people followed too,
And many cried and beat their chests
As anguished folk will do.

As they approached her father's hut
He heard all the commotion,
And when he saw Griselda there,
His heart burst with emotion.

He took the tattered overcoat
That she had worn before
From off its peg where it had hung
Behind the battered door.

The old man tried to wrap it round
His sad, mistreated child,
He felt that she'd been badly used,
Mishandled and defiled.

He'd always felt the marriage was
A very bad mistake,
He'd only gone along with it
For his dear daughter's sake.

And now she'd come back home to him –
And wouldn't say a word
About her marriage, her old life
And all that had occurred.

She lived with all humility –
And not in any way
By words or by expression or
By action – did display

That she believed she had been wronged
Or dealt with selfishly,
It seemed that she was quite resolved
To just let matters be.

At this point the good Clerk sighed,
He said, 'As you can tell
The sweet girl kept on smiling –
Despite all that befell.

'And though within these times of ours
Women get scant praise,
It must be said their constancy
Has power to amaze.

'With all my heart I do profess,
And very humbly say
There's not a man that's ever lived
Would act in such a way.

'No good sirs, there is no doubt
That the ladies do
Such things that many fellows don't –
For they act straight and true!'

The children of the Marquis now
Arrived at his great court,
They entered through its mighty gate
Along with their escort.

The Marquis when he saw them sent
A messenger to say,
'Griselda must attend at court,
She must come right away.'

So dutifully, as we'd expect
Griselda knelt before
The Marquis, and she wondered what
He might now have in store.

He spoke and said, 'My bride has come,
The girl whom I'm to wed,
And I need someone who is calm
And who can keep her head,

'To organise the rooms and all
The feasting and the fun,
And you Griselda, know of course
Just how I like things done.'

She replied, 'It's my delight
To gladly do your will,
If I were old and quite worn out,
My Lord, I'd serve you still.

'And be assured, I'll do all this
Until my final breath,
I'll only cease from serving you
When I, my Lord, meet death.'

And so she ordered everything,
And as the guests arrived
She welcomed them with friendliness
And selflessly contrived

To make them all as comfortable
As folk could ever be,
And even treated his new 'bride'
With all civility.

A sumptuous feast was organised,
And when the court was seated,
Griselda having ordered things
Now quietly retreated

To a place where she could see
That all was in control,
Where she could fuss and organise,
Remonstrate – cajole,

To make quite sure the banquet went
With an almighty swing,
'Twas at this point that 'cross the hall
A booming voice did ring.

It was the Marquis and he called
In jocular, loud tone,
He called a name so all could hear,
A name much loved and known.

'Griselda – where are you my sweet?'
He called, 'Griselda, dear.'
Griselda felt quite mortified.
He called, 'Come over here.'

As always her sweet face was calm
Though inside all ran rife.
The Marquis said, 'So tell me now,
How like you my new wife?

'Is she not most beautiful?
I beg you now to tell.'
Griselda feeling awkward said,
'I like her very well.

'In all my life I never saw
A lovelier, sweet girl,
And I can understand just why
Your heart is in a whirl.

'Why you have fallen for her sire,
And I will always pray
That you are happy – both of you,
Come whatever may.

'But may I ask but one small thing?
For I can clearly see
That she's been raised by gentlefolk
And not known poverty.

'So treat her kindly my dear Lord,
Not as I've seen you do
With others – even though they were
Extremely kind to you.'

She said all this without a trace
Of rancour – like a friend,
The Marquis came to clearly see
Her goodness had no end.

And then he spoke. 'This is enough.
Griselda dear, my wife,
You have suffered so much pain,
Distress and hurt and strife.

'You have shown throughout the years
You truly are the best,
For all this time I've heartlessly
Been putting you to test.

'And you have proved to be so true,
Through awful strife – whatever,
And you have shown such constancy
In your each endeavour.

'And by our Saviour, Christ the Lord,
I swear upon my life,
You are my one and only spouse,
You are my dearest wife.

'And this young lady here who stands
So lovely by my side
Is not who you suppose she is,
For she is not my bride.

'She is your daughter whom you thought
Died all those years ago,
And here's your son – your dear sweet boy
You can now get to know.

'I sent them to Bologna where
They've lived for all these years.'
Griselda swooned amid a pool
Of happy, anguished tears.

The Marquis said when she came round,
'I put you to the test,
To prove your goodness and dear wife
You've shown you are the best.'

Oh what a sight to see – it was
A most heart-rending scene,
The Marquis freely did admit
How devious he'd been.

Griselda though could hardly speak
So massive was her joy,
She wrapped her arms around her girl
And hugged her handsome boy.

And while her arms enveloped them
She fainted once again,
Her happiness was so intense
'Twas tantamount to pain.

What merriment was in the air
And what a feast that day,
As everything now ended in
This unexpected way.

The Marquis now was reconciled
With Griselda there,
And he resolved he never would
Set her another snare.

They lived for many happy years
In perfect, close accord,
Their loving daughter married then
A handsome, wealthy Lord.

Griselda's ageing father too
Was brought to live at court,
And though the time that he had left
Was quickly running short,

He spent his last years happily
Surrounded by much love
Till finally he died and went
To Heaven up above.

The handsome boy, Griselda's son
One day became the heir
To his proud father's grand estate
And lived with much joy there.

And when he married – happily
I can in all truth tell
That he was kindly to his wife
And treated her most well!

'And so my friends,' the Clerk then said,
'I haven't told this tale
To preach that women should submit
To this kind of travail.

'Few women could thus tolerate
All that Griselda bore,
If they but suffered half as much,
'Twould be the final straw.

'But even so, a moral lurks
Within this tale – and so
I urge you all to listen well
And heed this as you go.

'For we should all be most resolved
And quite prepared to be
Strong and steadfast, like a rock
Against adversity.

'Just like Griselda, for if she
Can be that strong and true
When tested by a man – well, friends,
This is my humble view,

'When tested by the Lord above –
We should without complaint,
Each and every one of us
Behave just like a saint.

'And one more word I'd like to say.
That is, I'm of a mind,
To say with certainty – you'd not
In any town now find

'A girl who's of Griselda's ilk,
They don't exist these days,
They've all got fancy ideas now
And very different ways.

'Well that's me done and so I think
Before we have some food,
I'd like to make you smile my friends
And change our sombre mood.

'So if you will permit me now,
As we all go along,
I'll liven up our company
And sing a little song!'

'For married men it's all the same,
It's mainly grief and pain.'

THE MERCHANT'S PROLOGUE

The Merchant who'd not said that much
Until this point, chimed in,
He looked around at all of us
And said with watery grin,

'I'm also married and must say
Like many of you here
That marriage hasn't proved to be
Much fun for me, I fear.

'It's all been weeping, wailing, strife,
And not much wedded bliss,
But then I guess that's how it goes,
For I must tell you this,

'My wife is quite a dragon –
I swear upon my life,
A fiend would come out worst if he
Were coupled with my wife.

'She's so unlike Griselda there,
She's cruel and very mean,
And anyone can see straight off
That she's no beauty queen.

'If I were single once again
I surely would beware,
For my old crone would not entice
This fellow to her lair.

'For married men it's all the same,
It's mainly grief and pain
No, I can say with certainty
I wouldn't wed again.

'We've now been married but two months
And I have had enough,
So don't be taken in my friends
By that romantic stuff.

'And one thing I can say for sure
No bachelor could be
As miserable and put upon
And badly used as me.'

Our merry Host grimaced and said,
'God bless your noble heart,
But from all this you surely have
A tale you can impart.

'For you now know the pitfalls of
The holy wedded state,
So you kind sir, must surely have
A cracker to relate.'

'You whore, you strumpet, faithless wife.'

THE MERCHANT'S TALE

In Lombardy, there lived a knight
Of sixty – so quite old,
And he was still a bachelor –
But also I am told

That though he lived in single state
He had an appetite
For the ladies and with them,
He seemed to do all right.

But then as he reached sixty – he
At this late stage of life,
Decided that he'd like to find
Someone to be his wife.

'For marriage is a blissful state'
This ancient knight had cried.
'It is the proper way to live.
Like paradise,' he sighed.

'And I could face most anything
That life throws in my path,
If I could have a faithful wife
To share my home and hearth.'

And so this old and hoary knight
Called all his friends one day
To come to him and this is what
The old knight had to say.

'You know I'm getting on in years.
Truth is I'll soon be dead.
The grave, it beckons me – in fact
I'm at its edge,' he said.

And then he took a long, deep breath
And told them of his plan.
'I am determined – quite resolved
To be a married man.

'So dear friends I ask if you
Will help me to assuage
This lonely feeling – but please find
A girl of tender age.

'I do not want a wrinkled crone,
I want one young and pretty,
One that's fun to have around,
Intelligent and witty.

'Now I am in a hurry – so
As there are lots of you
You'll stand a better chance to find
A comely lass who'll do.

'But let me make it very clear,
I'll not wed with a crone,
If she's not less than twenty years
I'll stay here on my own.

'For these old hags, as you well know
Are up to any trick,
They wear a man to nothing and
Do it in half a tick.

'But you can mould a sweet young thing
As if she were hot wax,
And when once done, you surely could
Be calm of mind – relax.

'And anyway, to wed a hag
Could be a grave mistake.
What if I didn't fancy her?'
Said this lust-driven rake.

''Twould force me to adultery
And this would then propel
My soul, when I am dead into
The very depths of hell.

'No, on this point, I must be clear,
I'd sooner forego grog,
Or lose all that I own, or be
Eaten by a dog,

'Than marry with an ancient sort.
It just shall not be done,
For if I marry, I intend
To have, my friends – some fun!'

❦

This knight whose name was January
Had two brothers who
Came to see him and each gave
His honest point of view.

The first one – called Placebo
Said, 'My brother dear,
Your plan to take a wife is one
That surely brings us cheer.

'Your judgement always has been sound.
You are a prudent man.
And our dear Lord himself will be
Delighted with your plan.

'It shows you've got a heart of gold.
My word, upon my soul,
To take a sweet, young comely wife
Is such a worthy goal.'

The other brother, Justinus
Had listened quietly,
And then he said, 'Dear January,
Please give your ear to me.

'To choose a wife is difficult,
There's so much to beware,
It is an act that must be done
With skill and utmost care.

'You should find out at first, for sure
Is she a fraud or cheat,
Or possibly intemperate,
A drunk or indiscreet?

'Is she the type who nags all day,
A spendthrift or much worse,
The type who always wants her way
And is inclined to curse?

'Is she a brawler and a shrew.
A scheming, lying lynx.
A hussy and a fiery cat,
A tartar and a minx?

'Believe me brother, for I know
Of marriage – for my wife,
Has been the cause of so much pain
Distress and hurt and strife.

'Folk think I love my wife and that
We're always in a clinch,
But brother dear, I know and well
Just where my shoe does pinch.

'But anyway, do what you will
But all could end in tears,
For she might quickly tire of you.
My guess is in three years.

'For you are old and very soon
You will not satisfy
A young and lustful beauty when
In so-called bliss you lie.

'But that is all I have to say.
You still may go ahead,
And if you do – take no offence
From what I have just said.'

Old January listened then
He said, 'Now that's enough.
I do not give a toss and I'll
Hear no more of this stuff.

'Say what you like, I will get wed,
And I say, any man
Is not a friend, if he should try
To stop my marriage plan.'

And so that wanton, ancient knight
Spent every waking hour
Trying to decide which maid
He'd wed and then deflower.

Then finally he made his choice.
He made it on his own.
He found the girl that he would wed,
She and she alone.

He dreamt of her through every night
And I must say in truth,
His thoughts were of a lustful kind,
About her form and youth.

He thought she was adorable,
Good-hearted and most kind.
He saw but goodness, for of course
An old man's love is blind.

He called his friends and then declared
In happy, buoyant voice,
'I've found the most attractive girl.
I have now made my choice.'

He said, 'There is within the town
A lovely looking girl,
And I will freely here admit
She's got me all a-twirl.

'But I'm concerned about one thing
And so would like some aid.
It bothers me and could affect
My marriage to this maid.

'For if I marry her and then
I manage to thus capture
A state of perfect happiness,
A life of perfect rapture.

'Well what will happen when I die
For has it not been told
That we are only granted once
True rapture thus to hold?

'For if I find a paradise
While living here below,
I'll be denied that of our Lord's
When it's my time to go.'

His brother Justinus then sneered,
'You may find soon enough
That marriage isn't that much fun,
It can be pretty rough.

'This wife of yours could prove to be,
Once you're well in her grip
Your purgatory – an instrument
Sent down from God to whip.

'And you'll be the recipient –
So when it's time to go
Your soul will race to heaven like
An arrow from a bow.

'But there is nothing more to add,
So brother, have your will,
But this I promise, once you're wed
Your life will go downhill!'

And with these words Justinus left,
Placebo followed too,
For they both realised there was
No more that they could do.

And so the nuptials took place
On the appointed day
And January wed his bride
Whose Christian name was May.

Oh yes, and what a lot of bonds
Were signed between the pair.
For May took every chance to see
The covenants were fair –

Fair to herself that is, for she
Got him to sign away
All kinds of rights – she made quite sure
For marriage he would pay.

So they were wed and afterwards
Came the wedding feast.
The pair sat at the table like
The beauty and the beast.

For May was young and fresh and pure,
The knight was like a bear.
There was no doubt they really were
A most unlikely pair.

But January didn't think
That maybe just perchance,
He was too old for her – he sat
In a besotted trance.

Or to be more accurate
A trance just filled with lust
He couldn't wait for night to come –
For he was fit to bust.

He couldn't wait to see the back
Of all his wedding guests,
He viewed them as a nuisance now –
Annoyances and pests.

Meanwhile there was a person there
Whose heart was filled with woe,
His name was Damian – he was
The old knight's squire – and though,

He'd acted normally and served
The knight and his new bride,
He was in such a state that it
Was getting hard to hide

The feelings that now wracked his frame –
For he could not allay
The strong emotions that he felt
For lovely, youthful May.

In desperation then he thought,
'I'm going off my head.'
And so with crazy, lovelorn thoughts
He took himself to bed.

And there he wept and beat his chest,
And cried, 'Life isn't fair.'
And as he cries for lovely May,
For now, we'll leave him there.

At last night came – the guests had left
And so to bed they went,
Old January truly thought
His May was heaven sent.

He drew her to him, kissing her,
This stoked his lustful fires.
As for poor May, she only felt
His bristles like sharp briars.

He said, 'Now we are wed sweet May
I'll have what is my due,
There can be nothing sinful in
What man and wife will do.'

And so he set to with a will
And laboured all night long,
Happy in the knowledge that
Now wed, he did no wrong.

And as for May – what did she think
Of her old, mangy mate,
All hanging skin and shrunken neck,
Bent back and shiny pate.

Well not a lot, in fact she thought
His antics were a joke,
He was, she thought, a sorry case,
A poor, worn-out, old bloke.

Three days passed and then the knight
Sat eating at his board,
And May was there and dutifully
Sat calmly by her Lord.

Then January looked around
And noticed by and by
That Damian was absent and
He said with testy sigh,

'Where is the lad, is he still sick?'
The others standing there
Said, 'He's still ill, we think he's got
An illness that's quite rare.'

Old January looked askance
And said with heavy sigh,
'He is a first-class squire, I'd be
Upset if he should die.'

And then he said to lovely May,
'Now we have finished here,
We'll visit Damian and give
The lad a little cheer.

'You go first and tell the boy
I'll come to see him later.'
So May went off to visit with
The old knight's favourite waiter.

Some ladies of the court went too –
On entering the room
They found the lad just lying there,
A picture of such gloom.

Sweet May sat down upon his bed
And tried to cheer the squire,
On seeing her, his passion rose
Into a raging fire.

Some days before, the lovesick lad
Had scribed a heart-felt note,
It was addressed to lovely May,
And in this note he wrote

Of his dear love – and some of it
He even wrote in verse,
And then he'd placed it safely in
A little leather purse.

And now he gave dear May the purse,
With nervous catch of breath
For he knew that the purse contained
A sure and certain death.

He slipped it to her furtively,
None of the ladies saw.
He said, 'Don't breathe a word of this
Or I am dead for sure.'

She took the purse and hid it then,
And once she was alone
She read his words excitedly
With an ecstatic groan,

For now she saw she fancied him
And so resolved to go
And tend to him and secretly
She'd also let him know

His love for her would be returned –
And so she went to pay
Another visit on the squire
Upon that very day.

And while with him, she furtively
Slipped a note into
His bed and thought, 'It's up to him
To do what he will do.'

When later Damian read the note
It raised his hopes so high,
He leapt straight out of bed – there was
A twinkle in his eye.

His sickness had now disappeared.
He was as right as rain,
And he went back to waiting on
His master once again.

Now January loved to walk
Entirely on his own,
In a garden hidden by
A solid wall of stone.

It was his special pride and joy
And no-one else but he
Could enter through the little door –
He held the only key.

But when he married youthful May
He'd take her there as well,
And what they did, perhaps, in truth
I shouldn't really tell.

Sufficient then to say that they
Within his potting shed
Did all the self-same things they did
When they were in their bed.

So life went on most sweetly till
The fickle fates then struck,
And proved how even best-laid plans
Can quickly come unstuck.

For woe of woes – oh what a turn
Events then sadly took,
But as we know, misfortune too
Is written in life's book.

Just when our life is going well
It's often that we find
Things can go wrong – and thus it was –
For the old knight went blind.

Oh how he carried on and cried,
Just constantly boohooing,
But most of all, he was concerned
At what May might be doing.

For now he couldn't see her,
He felt such jealous fear
That she might be unfaithful, so
He always kept her near.

He'd place his hand upon her arm
To make quite sure she kept
Chaste and pure and close to him –
But how poor, sweet May wept.

For she loved youthful Damian
And wished that they could play
As lovers do – (you understand),
But couldn't find a way.

And then one day old January,
Who had grown very lax
Left the garden key and May
Imprinted it in wax.

Then Damian with utmost care
And very skilfully,
Produced a perfect replica
Of the treasured key.

And now it was the summer time
And January said,
'Let's go into the garden May
And play as if in bed.'

Quick as a flash the crafty May
Gave Damian a sign,
He understood immediately
And made a quick beeline

For the little garden gate,
Unlocked it and slipped in.
He hid behind a holly bush,
Emotions all a-spin.

Then poor, old sightless January
Took May and led her to
The garden where he spoke and said,
'One thing I must tell you.

'Be faithful to your husband and
There are three things you'll get.
The love of Christ – your honour too.'
And then his face looked set,

'And all my lands and everything
That my dear I own.
I'll leave it all for you to have,
For you and you alone.

'We'll draw the deeds up right away,
Just love me truly dear.'
And then he said, 'Let's walk a while.'
And held her very near.

But as they walked she lied and said,
'I fear too for my soul,
To go to heaven when I die
Is my great wish and goal.

'And so I'd never be untrue,
And if I were I'd say,
Put me to death most horribly –
For every day I pray

'To be a credit to you dear
And show such constancy,
For every day, I try my best
To make you proud of me.'

As she spoke, she saw the squire
Perched precariously
Amid the branches and the fruit
Of a large pear tree.

She motioned him to keep quite still
And mouthed, 'I've got a plan.'
For she was quite determined that
She would now have this man.

You will I'm sure have heard folk speak
Of Pluto who is king
Of Fairyland – and he's been known
To have a lethal sting.

For as all this was going on,
Well, Pluto watched as well,
And he thought all unfaithful wives
Deserved to go to hell.

And so he waited on events
And watched as devious May
Put into place her crafty plan
To have some fun that day.

She led her poor, blind husband to
The pear tree, where above
Crouched Damian, her heart's desire,
Her handsome beau, her love.

'Oh husband, I see lots of pears,'
She said with longing sigh.
'If I can't have one now, I swear
Your hungry wife will die.

'Oh, let me get one straight away
Or I just won't feel right.
Sometimes a woman can't control
Her healthy appetite.

'Let me climb upon your back
So I can get a pear.
If you will just stoop down like this
I'll use you as a chair.'

So January did as bid
And she climbed on his shoulder,
While up above young Damian's
Passions did a-smoulder.

And when that wanton Damian
Saw his lovely May
Beside him in the tree – well he
Then had his wicked way.

But as the two there carried on
Pluto's face turned black,
And in revenge he swiftly gave
The knight his lost sight back.

Of course the first thing that the knight
Was very keen to see
Was his dearest, darling wife,
Above him in the tree.

But looking up, with horror then
The knight did there espy
Just what his wife was doing and
He let out such a cry.

It was the kind a person makes
When somebody dies,
You should have heard his angry words,
His wailing and his cries.

'You whore, you strumpet, faithless wife.
You'll never be my heir.'
Young May, as calmly as you like
Said, 'Husband, why thus swear?

'For I was told, to cure your eyes
There was one thing to do,
And that was struggle in a tree
With someone else than you.

'And all I get for trying here
To be a wife so kind,
Are angry words and not your thanks
That you're no longer blind.'

'Struggle with a man,' cried he.
'I saw with my two eyes,
That he was having you – I'll not
Be taken in by lies.'

'Your eyesight's still not good,' she said.
'It will take time to be
Completely cured – and then you'll show
Your gratitude to me.

'I was merely being kind.
I did this all for you.
My dearest husband, be assured
I'd never be untrue.

'When someone wakes from sleeping – well
It takes a little time
To fully come around and be
Right back in their prime.

'And so it is with blindness too,
You can't expect to be
Back to normal right away,
For it takes time to see.

'You have to wait a day or two
When you've been blind so long,
And so dear husband now I hope
You'll see I've done no wrong.'

Well, silly January said,
'I'm sorry, darling May.
I didn't mean to slander you,
Forgive me, dear, I pray.'

And so she jumped down from the tree
And he caressed her hair
To make amends, for now he felt
He had been most unfair!

'So that's my tale,' the Merchant said.
'So gentlemen, beware,
Do not be taken in by maids
Who look naïve and fair.

'Just watch your step – be sensible
And don't be taken in.'
And then the Merchant added,
And with a cheeky grin,

'Just keep your eyes wide open
So you can clearly see,
And then a cuckold is a thing
With luck, you'll never be!'

'And truthfully it hurts my brain,
So let's let matters lie.'

EPILOGUE TO THE MERCHANT'S TALE

'Well God have mercy on us all,'
The Host said, 'What a prat
That old knight was – and heaven save
Us all from wives like that.

'Look at all the subtle tricks
That women play on men.
The crafty wiles they use are such
As are beyond our ken.

'The way they play their little games
The Merchant's tale has shown,
They are beyond most anything
That men have ever known.

'I have a wife as you're aware,
Regrettably, not young,
And she's renowned both far and wide
For her loud, blabbing tongue.

'Oh, and other vices too,
Too many here to tell,
But living with her all these years
I clearly know them well.

'I'll not recount them to you now
Though there are many more,
For what's the point in rubbing at
A painful open sore.

'And if I told you all her faults,
Well, then I know for sure
Each and every word I said
Would go back to our door.

'They always find out what you've said
And how you've done them wrong,
And as I have just pointed out,
The list would be too long.

'And truthfully it hurts my brain,
So let's let matters lie,
And anyway I'm stuck with her
Until the day I die.'

And to his famous court one day
There came a noble knight

THE SQUIRE'S TALE

Then once again our Host spoke out,
He said, 'What I desire
Is to hear a tale of love,
So tell us one, dear Squire.

'I would appeal to your goodwill
To speak about true love,
For it is my belief that you
Have knowledge far above,

'That of hen-pecked married men
Who wend their weary way
Predictably, along life's path,
Good fellow, what d'you say?'

'With pleasure, I will try my best,'
The friendly Squire replied.
'But do you truly, sir, believe
That I am qualified?'

But even so he soon began,
He spoke about a king
Called Cambuskan – who was a man
Well versed in everything.

And to his famous court one day
There came a noble knight.
He rode into the palace hall –
And what a wondrous sight.

He said he came from India
And brought from his grand Lord
Four gifts – a horse, a mirror,
A gold ring and a sword.

He told the king, 'This horse I bring
Was fashioned out of brass.
He needs no sustenance at all –
No water, hay or grass.

'And if you turn this little key
He'll take you anywhere,
To any country in the world
He'll fly you through the air.

'The mirror that I bring is not
Like any that you've seen,
For it can tell who is your friend
And show a future scene,

'To warn you of dire happenings
Which may affect your land,
And it will show who you can trust
To give a helping hand.'

The whole court gathered there just gasped
And stood intently gazing
At the gifts which truly were
Astounding and amazing.

Then the Knight held up the ring
And said, 'Whoever's hand
Shall wear this ring – will have the skill
To clearly understand

'The language of our feathered friends,
He'll have the gift to know
The perfect meaning of the notes
Of finch or hawk or crow.'

And then he grasped the mighty sword
And said, 'This blade will cut
Through any armour, it will slice
Through quite the toughest nut.

'And the wounds it makes will heal
If the blade is laid
Carefully upon the cut
The blade itself has made.'

What wondrous gifts these were for sure –
And then the young Squire told
Of how Cambuskan's daughter
Had left the great household,

And how she'd strolled within the woods
And on her finger there,
She'd worn the ring – and then she met
A falcon in despair.

The falcon had then told her
Of love that had gone wrong,
An unrequited love that was
So powerful and strong...

Then at this point, the Franklin spoke,
'My dear young sir and Squire,
You tell a tale in such a way
I readily admire.

'I have a son and dearly wish
That he could speak as you,
You've learnt the art of language sir,
You know it through and through.'

But sadly that was all we heard
Of those enchanting things
Of which the Squire had spoken – for,
We heard no more of kings,

Or magic horses, mighty swords,
Of mirrors and of rings,
Of falcons speaking soulful words
And all those clever things.

The Franklin's interruption
Had left us high and dry,
We never heard another word –
The Squire was too shy.

He didn't try to recommence
His most enchanting tale,
He seemed contented just to let
The Franklin's will prevail.

And as the Franklin was quite set
To tell a tale himself,
The Squire's tale was put back on
The storyteller's shelf.

And then the Franklin said, 'Good sirs,
I'm not a well-read man,
So please excuse the way I speak –
I'll do the best I can.

'I have no expertise with words,
Smart tricks I do not know,
I haven't delved into vast books
Or read great Cicero.

'The way I speak is plain and clear
With not one fancy frill,
For as you know, I do not have
Our good friend Chaucer's skill.

'But if you'll listen,' he declared
And with a little cough,
'I'll tell my tale – and do my best.'
The Franklin then set off.

She also saw the jagged rocks
When she gazed down below

THE FRANKLIN'S TALE

My tale is set in Brittany
And is about a knight
And the woman that he loved –
Such an enchanting sight.

She was of noble birth and she
Was of that special kind
That combines rare beauty with
A lively, gracious mind.

This knight – called Arveragus
Asked his love one day
If she'd consent to be his wife,
And then had this to say.

'If you become my wife, I'll not
Boss you around,' he said.
'Or act with jealousy – I'll show
I'm noble and well bred.'

The sweet, young girl called Dorigen
Said, 'For such courtesy
I'll be a faithful, loving wife
To you my Lord – you'll see.'

And so they made their love-filled pact
Both of the same accord
That he would treat her with esteem
And she'd respect her Lord.

In no time they were wed and he
Took his new bride back home,
But 'twas not long before the knight
Felt a need to roam.

For after spending but a year
In happy, wedded bliss,
He said, 'To Britain I must go.'
And with a parting kiss,

He left his dear wife Dorigen,
But said, 'I'll soon return.'
For though within his heart, the fires
Of fervent love did burn,

He was intent to seek out deeds
Of chivalry and so
To Britain to earn honour he
Was now resolved to go.

When he had gone, sad Dorigen,
Wept and pined so much,
She missed his smile, his company,
His kind support and touch.

And though she grieved unhappily
In her isolation,
One small thing kept her buoyed up
And brought her consolation.

For Arveragus wrote to her
And said time and again,
'I'll soon be home,' and his kind notes
Helped to relieve her pain.

Her friends tried hard to make her smile
And though they didn't fuss,
Quite often they would say to her,
'Please come and walk with us.'

And so she then began to stroll
Along the rampart wall
Which overlooked the sea – she heard
The wailing seagulls call,

And crashing foam and winds – but then
As she went to and fro
She also saw the jagged rocks
When she gazed down below.

They looked so dark and dangerous,
Forbidding and severe,
They surely threatened any ship
That ventured to go near.

She'd sigh and then muse to herself
As she stood taking stock,
'They say all has a purpose but
Why has God made this rock?

'It seems to make but little sense.
Wherever is the gain?
And yet they say the Lord above
Makes nothing here in vain.

'These rocks bring no real benefit,
They only cause mayhem,
So many poor, doomed, stricken souls
Have lost their lives on them.

'No bird or beast gains anything,
These rocks just cause alarm,
The only thing they ever do
Is bring good folk to harm.'

And then as she looked down she shed
A single, soulful tear
As she thought of her husband who
Had now been gone a year.

It was the month of May and so
A picnic dance was planned,
With sumptuous food and drink for all
And a fiddling band.

The gardens where this all took place
Were colourful and nice,
A riot of the brightest hues,
A mini paradise.

And once the feasting had been done
They all began to dance
Except for Dorigen who sat
In an unhappy trance.

If only her dear husband could
Have been with her that day,
Then she'd have felt complete – things would
Have gone a different way.

For in amongst the dancers there
Was one who had the name,
Aurelius – a lusty squire,
And flirting was his game.

He was a jolly kind of cove
And very handsome too,
And all could see he danced with style
When he came into view.

He had a pleasant way and he
Was affluent as well,
And Dorigen had charmed this lad –
He'd fallen 'neath her spell.

For when he first caught sight of her
Cupid had shot his dart,
And from that moment, Dorigen
Had owned the squire's heart.

And now he looked at her and thought,
'I'd love to be her beau.'
And then he thought, 'Perhaps it's time
For me to let her know.'

And so approaching her he said,
'Madam, hear me, pray,
I love you dearly and I beg
Don't spurn this love today.'

'What,' she cried, 'I can't believe
You'd say these words to me,
For I'm a married lady – so
I'm certainly not free.

'And I would never, ever be
A false, disloyal wife,
I swear this by the Lord above
Who gave my being life.'

But then she said mischievously
Just from a sense of fun,
'I might grant you my love, if sir
One thing you could get done.

'Along the coast of Brittany
There's so much rock and stone,
As I am sure that you're aware
For this fact is well known.

'And many vessels perish there –
And so I say to you,
If you can find a way to change
This most depressing view,

'If you can fashion a design
To take the rocks away
So that our ships can safely dock,
Well, I'm prepared to say,

'If this great feat you can achieve –
By our good Lord above,
Why in return I'll give you sir
My true, undying love.'

'Is this the only way to win
Your precious heart?' he said.
'Yes,' she replied, 'so put all thoughts,
Of loving from your head.

'This deed is quite impossible
And I insist good sir,
To lust for someone else's wife
Marks you out a cur.'

So Aurelius went back home,
A beaten, sorry man,
He was distraught and overcome
By failure of his plan.

He went to bed and felt so bad
He thought that he was dying,
He spent the whole of each long day
Just calling out and sighing.

He prayed there for a miracle,
To make the rock and stone
Disappear – so that her love
He could claim as his own.

And as he lay there wearily,
His only consolation
Was the comfort and support
Of a close relation.

His brother tried his best to give
Advice and to dispense
An ample dose of sympathy
And also common sense

To Aurelius – for he knew
About the failed affair.
He tried to lift his brother from
The depths of his despair.

And then the brother had a thought,
He cried out loud, 'Of course!'
The idea hit his being with
An overpowering force.

For way back in his student days
He'd had a passing look,
At a quite enormous tome,
A most mysterious book.

It told of clever conjurors
Who caused immense confusion
By making people see strange things
That were but an illusion.

Sometimes they'd conjure up a lion
Or fill a hall with water,
Or show a mighty castle keep
Made out of bricks and mortar.

And then they'd make them disappear
Into some other zone,
So maybe someone had the power
To deal with rock and stone.

He thought, 'If I could find a chap
Who had the skill to make
All beholders struck with awe –
Someone with skill to fake.

'Who could make all the rocks and stone
That lie along our shore
Disappear – or leastways seem
As if they are no more.

'Then everything would be all right,
My brother would recover,
For he could tell fair Dorigen
That she must be his lover.'

He spoke then to Aurelius
And said, 'You look so thin,
But I believe I have the power
To cure the state you're in.

'We'll go to Orléans town and find
A special kind of man.'
And then he told his brother of
His very clever plan.

So off they went and when they reached
The outskirts of the town
Towards the end of that long day,
Just as the sun went down,

They met a fellow who spoke out
In Latin – loud and clear,
And he amazed them for he said,
'I know just why you're here.'

He said, 'Let's walk on to my home
And we can have a chat,
For I know what is on your mind,
I know just where you're at.'

And so they joined the fellow who –
As they sat down to eat –
Struck them dumb for he performed
The most amazing feat.

For right before their very eyes
He caused then to appear
A forested and lush green park
Inhabited with deer.

And then he showed another scene
Of knights so bold and brave
Jousting with each other – then
The wizard gave a wave,

And there before their very eyes,
Sweet Dorigen they saw,
She danced – and then the wizard waved
And she was there no more.

So Aurelius was convinced
The wizard had the skill
To make the rocks all disappear,
So he could thus fulfil

The end his heart desired so much,
With Dorigen to lay,
But to achieve all this – how much
Would he be asked to pay?

They haggled back and forth until
The wizard said, ''Twill be
A thousand crowns for me to move
The rocks of Brittany.'

Aurelius just laughed with joy
And soundly clapped his knee.
'A thousand crowns, if that's the price,
I readily agree.'

And so to Brittany they went,
The brothers and the wizard,
'Twas now the season of the snow,
Of frost and storm and blizzard.

The wizard quickly set to work,
He laboured with a will.
He paid no heed to snow or sleet
Or to the wind's cold chill.

But carefully he watched the time
For the grand conclusion
Of his work – he judged the hour
To make his grand illusion.

Did he use skulduggery
Or evil spirits or
Astrology – and science too
Or did he use all four?

We'll never know – but still he toiled,
He watched the waning moon,
And then he told Aurelius,
''Twill happen very soon.'

By day and night Aurelius,
With stomach in a knot
Waited, wondering if he would
Secure his love or not.

And then it happened – what a thing,
A miracle for sure,
For there was not a single rock
On Brittany's wild shore.

Aurelius fell onto his knees
And told the wizard this,
'You've turned my life from deep despair
Into a state of bliss.'

And then he set off hurriedly
To Dorigen to say,
'The rocks of Brittany are gone,
I've come to have my way.'

He found her in the temple and
He took her by the hand
And said, 'Where all the rocks once stood
Is now just golden sand.

'Look for yourself and you will see
I have fulfilled the task
That you decreed would earn your love –
So now I come to ask

'That you fulfil the promise made
Within the garden for
I only wish for you to do
That which you pledged – no more.'

He left her then but boldly said,
'My love – I will return.'
But let us linger there for we
Will sadly then discern

The great distress that tore at her –
She cried in grief and woe,
She remonstrated with herself
And shook from head to toe.

'How could a miracle like this
Ever come to be.
It means I'll lose my honour or
'Twill be the death of me.

'And in truth I'd rather die
Than lose my honest name,
Since if I honour his demand
I only die of shame.

'Best to take my life myself
Like others in the past.'
The more she thought – the more convinced
She was the die was cast.

For three long days she wept and wailed
Borne down with many fears,
Then Arveragus came back home,
He said, 'Why all these tears?

'Are you not pleased to see your spouse
Who's been away so long?
Please tell my dear, my darling wife,
What in the world is wrong?'

So Dorigen told everything
And when her husband heard
Of what she'd promised – he then said,
'You must, dear, keep your word.

'Of all the things that we possess,
The truth remains supreme,
For it is this and this alone
That warrants our esteem.

'So you must go and say to him,
You'll honour what you said.'
Then he broke down and wept and wished
He and his wife were dead.

He said, 'Go to him now, but don't
Speak of this grave affair,
If ever it should come to light
'Twould be too hard to bear.

'But go my wife and see this man,
Do what you said you'd do.'
And so she left and quickly then
She disappeared from view.

And when she saw Aurelius,
She said with great despair,
'My husband bade me come to you
To honour this affair.'

Aurelius was astounded
And stunned by what she said.
To think the noble knight had sent
His wife to share his bed.

He did this out of honour and
A sense of what was right.
Aurelius was humbled by
These words and by the sight,

Of Dorigen just standing there,
A broken, stricken girl.
His gallant side, his better side
Began then to unfurl.

And so he said, 'Please tell your Lord
I'm sorry for this mess,
And tell him I apologise
For causing him distress.

'I see he is a noble man
And so I tell you now,
I give you back to him and will
Release you from your vow.

'I'll never bother you again,
You are the noblest wife
That I have ever come across
In all my misspent life.'

She fell down on her knees with thanks,
Then went back to her knight,
And oh what happiness they felt
That things were now all right.

And they pursued their happy life
On Brittany's fair shore –
Of this contented couple now
We need know nothing more!

So back to young Aurelius,
His life has turned to rubble
For he still owes the thousand crowns
So this spells out some trouble.

For he can't pay the debt right now
As he's been rather rash.
He'd thought that in his coffers he
Had stored a larger stash.

So now he's faced with ruin if
The wizard wants his dough,
Not in instalments, but right now –
Straight off – all in one go.

And so he gathered what he had
And then went off to see
What kind of deal he could work out
And hopefully agree.

He told the wizard, 'I am short
Of ready funds right now.
But I'll repay it all to you,
You have my solemn vow.'

The wizard said, 'I ask you sir,
Did I not keep my side?
For truthfully did I not make
The mighty rocks subside?

'And that young lady – did you not
Then have your way with her.'
'No, no,' Aurelius replied,
'That, sir, did not occur.'

Then he told the wizard how,
To honour what was right,
Her husband had agreed that she
Should come to him that night.

'But I took pity, for I saw
She hadn't thought her vow
Would land her in this awful mess,
She couldn't see just how

'You could remove those rocks which were
Such a great protrusion,
For she knew nothing of your arts,
Of magical illusion.

'So that, good sir, is all there is,
There's nothing more to know,
For I released her from her vow
And then I let her go.'

The wizard nodded prudently
And then he did proclaim,
'You are a squire and he a knight
Yet acted both the same.

'With kindness and nobility,
Though both have been upset,
The one did honour – one release
The other from a debt.

'So I can surely do the same,
The rules I too can bend,
For I release you from your debt,
You're in the clear, my friend.

'And now the coast is clear of rocks,
And so, good sir, I say,
This benefit to all mankind
Will be sufficient pay.'

And then without another word
He mounted his fine bay,
With head held high, no backward glance
The wizard rode away.

The Franklin sighed and said, 'Well now,
My tale has reached its end.
I wonder which of these three chaps
You'd most want as a friend.

'Each acted very reasonably,
Behaved both straight and true.
Who was the finest gentleman?
I'd like to hear your view.

'They acted with humility
And each rejected vice,
So which one do you think thus made
The greatest sacrifice?'

And so the Franklin left us all
To ponder and discuss
Which one of these three gentlemen
Appealed the most to us.

But as we talked a cry went up,
Of course it was our Host.
'Praise the Lord and all his works –
And let's all drink a toast,

'And mark this special moment – yes
And sanctify this hour,
For there, if you look through those trees
You'll see a massive tower.

'And there upon that very spot
Is where our journey ends,
For that is Canterbury and
Good Beckett's shrine, my friends.'

And so we made our way towards
The great cathedral where
Our pilgrimage would end and we
Would kneel in humble prayer.

But not surprisingly, our Host
Pronounced the final word,
Of course we knew he'd want to speak
On all that had occurred.

He said, 'I thank you kindly
For first including me,
And then for your companionship
And friendly company.

'And I must say, we've had some fun
And frolics on the way,
And honestly, I do confess
That I've loved every day.

'The funny jokes and little jibes,
The banter and the wit.
What can I say, dear friends, I've loved
Just every little bit.

'Oh and yes, the tasty food
And trying all the ales,
But I must say that most of all
I've loved your merry tales.

'I'll not forget them, that I won't,
They'll always stay with me.'
And then he threw his hat up high
And shouted out with glee.

'You're all my friends, I love you all,
Each and every one,
But now our happy pilgrimage
Is very nearly done.

'And we can say in future life,
Whatever may befall,
That we have been to Canterbury,
So bless us one and all!'

And then he turned his horse and rode
Towards the tower – full pelt,
And everyone of us I'm sure
Knew how our good Host felt.

For we had reached our journey's end,
And what a special day
For soon we'd be at Beckett's shrine
And there we'd kneel and pray.

And then renewed and fortified
We would retrace our way,
Back to the Tabard Inn to where
It all began that day.

But not a person there would e'er
Forget what he had done,
For it had been quite wonderful
And such tremendous fun!

'*It's time to say farewell my friends –*
It's time for me to go.'

CHAUCER'S FINAL WORD

Well this is now the end and if
You have enjoyed these tales
Then praise the Lord and all his works –
His goodness never fails.

But if you found you did not like
My humble efforts here,
Well fair enough but be assured
My motives were sincere.

If anything offended you
It was not my intention,
But if it did then I'm to blame –
For all was my invention.

I did my best and it was not
My aim to thus displease,
So put it down to just my lack
Of proper expertise.

But now I've done, you've heard the tales
That we all told and so
It's time to say farewell my friends –
It's time for me to go.

But think of Geoffrey Chaucer
And please I beg extol
The virtue of my tales and pray
For my eternal soul.

And if you dwell on me perhaps
You'll feel a warmth – and then
You'll shed a tear or maybe smile
And with me say – Amen.